ROMA

by
Aldo
Palazzeschi

translated
by
Mihaly
Csikszentmihalyi

Henry Regnery
Company CHICAGO

ROMA

139069

ROMA

VIA DI
MONSERRATO

FROM ONE side of the Farnese
Palace a poor and stately street forsaken by wealth winds its
way with the movement of a snake up to Santa Lucia. Its buildings show on their faces the stern sadness of decaying nobility.
Their portals, dark during the day as if they had become insen-
sitive to the Roman sun, are in the evening faintly illuminated
by lights of chilling weakness. And as diurnal noises, muted
by the walls, slowly abate, a voice hoarsened by wine shivers
under their arches, telling of floods and landslides, of air, land
and sea disasters, fires, gas leaks, explosions, collapsing buildings, bloodsheds and crimes of unheard of, yet believable,
cruelty.

1

"Wife shoots husband dead on Vittorio Boulevard," shouts the man who sells the evening papers. The voice is now warmer, as it spreads out like the sound of a bell.

"Good for her!" answers an old woman crossing the street; she holds to her breast a bottle of milk with the grace of a lily—"he must have deserved it," she confidently adds.

"She is a son-of-a-bitch an' a whore," the newspeddler stops indignantly, straightening his crumpled body, "that's what she is."

The old woman doesn't answer. She walks away in silence, with the white bottle close to her breast; what she wanted to say she did say, and that satisfies her.

On Saturday evenings peace is over the earth, the elements are at rest, even hostile nature is on mankind's side. No cataclysms, no crimes or conflicts, no blood, everything proceeds as on the edge of a sword, man's heart is open to joy and hope.

"Complete results of the Lottery," shouts the peddler with unshrinkable conviction, and in the month of June he may add, in lower case, the results of the bicycle races.

Only children can resist the oppression and charm of the street; they merrily play among its walls and on the little square about its middle. Where do they come from, whose are the children one sees on the deserted squares and working-class streets of this city? They come and go, leaving the impression of insects swarming, of migrating birds, of fleeing mice. . . . Under such gracious skies families let their children go out on the street perhaps with only a warning to watch out for cars, and vicariously enjoy an hour of true freedom, more than just the hour of quiet which follows in the narrow home. It is a small society going about its business almost unnoticed and uncurbed within the large, tired and worried one; it is the time when men enjoy a purity which later will be lost and whose memory

2

will become more beautiful as life hurries on. The children of the Roman people appear everywhere with the bold ease of wild flowers. The wind decreed their being, and they are proud of their station, not noticing its discomfort even if it is the most uncomfortable. It isn't easy to distinguish which are the children of really poor people and which of parents who enjoy a tolerably modest tenor of life. Some dress decently, others show inborn taste even in their poverty, and during the good season, which is the longest, they aren't dressed at all; nothing seems to cover the small pink bodies in perpetual motion blending with the enveloping light.

To the sons of the middle class such happiness is not permitted; to them the life of the streets is closed. They walk through them chaperoned, with superior and proper glances; at the sight of their unchained mates they suppress a twinge of envy.

After the age of twelve they leave the street; even those who as children seemed poorest now wear well-tailored suits with long trousers, a shirt and a tie, and they return to it as common pedestrians of that other Society, not condescending even to glance at their replacements in the lesser one, whose memory lives hidden in their hearts. Their voice is precociously masculine, and they can articulate it with inborn art, with a sensitivity developed from the music of the language, with a flowery grace that runs the range from persuasive tones of tenderness to the whiplash of vulgar and offensive words. The tender bodies moving so swiftly and unnoticed among adults assume very early the latter's timbre, silhouette and gait.

Something is distracting a group of them, for it's obvious that they don't concentrate on the game, and once in a while they interrupt it to look at the corner where the street enters the square.

Half an hour ago a little old man all dressed in black left the most ancient of those palaces. His round red face carried the memory of the countryside. Under his arm he held a folded

3

canvas satchel. Every morning the little man in black leaves those gates with the worn satchel under his arm, to return half an hour later holding it officiously, hanging by its handle. Only the different way of carrying it lets one suspect that there must be something inside, otherwise it still looks empty. He has been at Campo dei Fiori to do his unsubstantial shopping.

The children know him only too well, and looking through him with angelic hypocrisy they turn around to continue their games, demonstrating perfect disinterest in their behavior, which is made of interest only. And still with their backs turned they notice the reaction on the old man's face, a close-mouthed smile that cuts his face, which looks like an apple bitten by a child, feigning a menace turned not against them, but perhaps against the air.

He goes about in the fashion of web-footed birds, placing his foot flat at each step, moving his body with the intimate pleasure of tasting the ground as he walks.

This morning is a special one. The exact nature of its secret was read by the children in the caution with which the old man had left the house, and in the menacing cast of his mouth at his return.

The group of boys gets larger. Although the others try hard to chase the new ones away, they seem to materialize from the street.

"What do you want?"

"Nothing."

"Then why don't you go away?"

"I like it here, that's why."

"Stinker."

"Ass."

They gather with untruthful carelessness to go even if not called. With formal shyness they follow the old man at a respectful distance, as if they were expecting to be invited, while underneath they feel ready for much braver challenges.

The housekeeper has come to the door:

"Mister Checco."

"Missbice."

Gray hair smooth over the temples gives an air of severity to her figure already impressive in a clerical robe. She has come out to see the spectacle that will follow.

Reaching the entrance, Mister Checco turns suddenly, pretending surprise at the sight of the band gathered at his footsteps, ready to scare them away. But the boys move closer together to strengthen the entering wedge.

"If you think you are coming in to raise hell I'll throw you out on your ears. And who are you?"

"He's my cousin," the boy next to him answers sharply.

"Anyway, the more of you there are the less you'll get," concludes the little man in black with the sullen red face. The others hang their heads, resigned to brotherly sharing. Mister Checco, who knows almost every one of them, looks them all over to see whether there have been some unlawful infiltrations. There are about twenty, all from that street.

"There isn't that much stuff . . . we don't have a factory here."

From the pocket of the worn-out overcoat he takes out a large key and walks to the last door of the portal toward the court of the palace. The turning of the key in the rusted lock produces an orchestral movement in the children's eyes; the unpleasant sound wakes deep memories in each of them. Mister Checco hardens, knowing that at certain times kindness has to be hidden. The room is divided from the courtyard by a frightening iron gate; in the middle of it a huge table stands surrounded by benches so bored by insects that they have become intolerant of any weight for even the shortest time. On the walls are two paintings the subjects of which would

5

have been useless to investigate; lost in darkness, their gilded frames are covered by a black patina.

The boys throng around the table. In its center are some papers resembling shirts that have been used so often that they have become obscene. One knows that underneath there must be extremely tasty things which take pleasure in flaunting the monastic air of the room—a contrast which the children underscore with eyes quivering from unrestrainable greed. Someone tries to push over his neighbor to secure a better place at the table's edge. The one pushed lets go with his elbow.

"You can't stay here."

"Why?"

"Because you are a son of a whore."

"That's what *you* say."

He does not exactly know what a whore is, otherwise he wouldn't be so offended.

"You are a son of a whore and an ass."

"And you have no balls."

Mister Checco, ready to lift the first shirt, has an automatic awakening of authority.

"You say that word again and out that door you go with a kick in your behind."

They are sizzling with impatience and to shorten the wait they put up submissive faces.

After unveiling a venison pie shining in aspic and nailed with black truffles, Mister Checco uncovers a cake dressed in snow-white sugar, ribs of gold and silver, with "Merry Christmas" written across the middle.

If the first may seem a tower, the second resembles a dome—masterpieces of the culinary art that are prepared for gala dinners and great occasions.

With the look of a good shepherd, Mister Checco is about to divide the papers into as many sheets as there are lambs

6

in his flock. He looks them over one at a time, asking of their impatience the last effort, the most difficult; then brandishing a metal spatula he begins to divide the prodigious objects to give each his due.

Pupils are in constant rotation, elbows move by themselves as if larger space next to the table should entail a larger share. Eyes and elbows are joined by tongues which appear and disappear with flashes of coral between the lips. Each offers his piece of paper which in imagination enlarges to become the size of a tablecloth.

Mister Checco starts distributing the venison pie, then the splendid cake which slowly lets its poetic shape fall. The boys' eyes run from the one to the other with electric speed. It seems that all are suffering from the most cruel injustice and have to make some claims, while Mister Checco, on whose cheeks the wrinkle deepens in the roundness of the face, shows himself ever more convinced of his own equity.

"I'll take it to my mother."

"You say that so he will give you more."

"But they are brothers," someone tries to exclude another.

"If they are brothers don't they have two mouths just the same?"

The operation is accomplished. The wide trays are, except for a few leftovers, empty in the center of the table that looks monastic again, and Mister Checco, gathering the crumbs of what was the cake, pops them in his mouth with the hollow of his hand.

"Goody, goody," he tells the children, more to justify their gluttony than to satisfy his own. Ready to take flight they turn toward the door that Mister Checco goes to open slowly, holding in their arms the precious parcels.

"Greetings to mother," he tells the oldest one, who leaves last.

"Today we are going to see the Infant Jesus; I am going to

7

take them with me," he turns to the other children protectively, as if the holiday of innocence belonged to the smaller ones rather than to himself.

"I am going to go there today, too," adds Mister Checco with a tone that is more childish than the boy's. Traversing the portal they scatter on the street like swallows in air.

Mister Checco lifts from one of the benches his satchel, the only weight that the patient could tolerate without complaint, and closes the door again on the completed effort. The grinding of the key inside the lock calls out the housekeeper for the second time.

"Mister Checco."

"Missbice."

Weightless, the rosy old man ascends the staircase of the palace on which the hint of a constantly gray light trickles down from a window as large as it is stingy. Reaching the second floor in front of a strikingly tragic door, he takes from the pocket of his small coat a second key much larger than the first, enormous, which he handles with surprising familiarity; with no less ease he enters a dark and endless hall, entirely empty, frightening. The four windows that face Via Monserrato have surrendered, unable to make light. Against the main wall, at the top of five steps covered with red carpet, stands a golden throne under an immense purple canopy: trimmings and plaits form in its center the papal coat of arms. There, by ancient privilege of the family, the Pope deigned to sit in times past.

Having crossed the limitless hall with the step of one who is completely master of the desert, the old man walks into the next room, a much smaller one, and very much darker because lit by one window only. In its middle stands erect a man with hands behind his back, six-foot-two tall, a pale face and nobly equine head. His pallor illuminates the half-shadows; his all-black clothes suggest under the skin a skeleton of extraordinary

8

shape and size. Above a high celluloid collar, and below a head rich in still not all-white hair, the large black eyes are set in concave cheeks; like precipices they attract and repel at the same time. His hands are locked behind the back stooped at the shoulders not by age, but by the weight of his frame.

"Have you given the children Norina's things?"

"Yes, Excellency." Without looking at his questioner the little old man crosses the room with even steps.

"They keep making fun of the foundling who stays with the cobbler, they call him son of a whore, these things they hear from the grown-ups. If I hear you again you won't set foot inside here no more, I told the one who said it."

"Was Gasperina's little boy there?"

"Yes, Excellency."

"And those of Lucia?"

"Now, because those are brothers they wanted me to give them only one share. That's a good one. If they are brothers they are supposed to have one mouth among them."

These words are spoken by the round little man as he crosses the second room, talking to the air. He does not change his step either in front of the huge all-crimson throne, or the impressive all-black figure of the Prince of Santo Stefano, whom he passes by as the second monument of the house.

In that room His Excellency had collected all household necessities: the narrow iron bed with a white blanket for the nightly rest of the widowed Lord, on the side a *prie-dieu* on which triumphs a silver cross that an ancestor took home from a Crusade; the dresser and the desk on which stands a second crucifix, this one of ivory; a large vestry chest; and along the front wall a black leather sofa and two ancient armchairs of the same material. That room and the hall with the papal throne is what remains to him of his palace, and from there

9

he directs every action of his life. Behind these Checco has set up a tiny kitchen and a closet for his lair.

As soon as day comes—in the gray of morning's first light, during winter in full darkness—the two black shapes leave the palace: one very tall and thin, the other small and roundish; they leave through the small hatch carved inside the panes of the huge door. Although their legs are different, Checco follows one step behind without emphasizing the rhythm of his body, with ease, as a duck accustomed to walking with a horse. His Excellency assists the first Mass in the poor church of Santa Lucia, his parish. At the end of the service, the priest gives communion. His assistant, kneeling at the side of the altar, recites the *confiteor*. Whoever has heard Don Filippo di Santo Stefano recite that prayer of sorrow and contrition will not forget his voice at the *mea culpa, mea culpa, mea maxima culpa*, when he strikes his breast. The faithful hide their faces in their hands, on the verge of crying. Having given the host to his assistant, the priest goes on to give communion to the others, while the Prince holds under each one's chin the small silver tray. First to be given communion is Checco. There is no exception to this rule, and woe to the unwary who tries to take that place which by implicit right belongs to him, for he might start an argument inside the church.

Leaving Mass in full daylight the two black figures separate. The Prince is off to the Congregation of Saint Vincent de Paoli, the charitable organization of which he is head, and where he spends most of the day; Checco goes back to the household chores. By the time he returns the large door is already open, and he exchanges the ritual greeting with the housekeeper.

"Mister Checco."

"Missbice."

And he leaves a few hours later with the canvas satchel folded under his arm.

About two o'clock, when the Prince is back from the Congregation or some other charity, he sits at the round table in the center of the room, and Checco brings on the soup. Then he carries in his own plate. Across the table from each other they begin to eat. After the soup they eat some vegetables or eggs, some cheese and a little fruit. The words they exchange during the meal are few and always the same, and they rarely look at each other. His Excellency usually appreciates what he eats: "The soup is exquisite, how good this cheese, these eggs are very good," he tells the servant, who in no way acknowledges the praise as if it was only his due; at the most he mumbles a word that can't be understood, or nods agreement with the opinion. The lunch becomes a true feast when on holiday eves they share a herring; then Checco eats bread endlessly with his half. On days like that one bun is not enough for him. The Prince too, although he eats less bread, finds it extremely appetizing. And they too have their extravagances. For the Prince it is a handful of dried olives, which he eats one at a time with truly aristocratic grace; observing him one wouldn't know whether the gesture or the fruit satisfies him more. And for Checco there is a dinner which comes close to sin: two slices of ham and a bunch of grapes. The only difference is that while the Prince drinks water, as he has from birth, the servant keeps for himself a glass of excellent wine. That too is a gift from Norina, who knows how much he likes it. In the evenings, after reciting the rosary, they drink coffee with cream at the same table, then go off to sleep in order to be up by five in the morning.

On high holidays, of which there are several during the year, master and servant leave together, Checco always on the right; in front of the palace waits a car with the plates: *Sacred City of the Vatican,* ready to take His Excellency, the Prince Filippo di Santo Stefano, Secret Chamberlain to His Holiness, to a solemn ceremony or function. United, at the distance of one step, a distance not imposed by any protocol but born from itself, pure, the two attend the same ceremony, the same function. In the church of Ara Coeli over the Capitol Hill, dressed in the cloth of Saint Francis, there is no distinction between master and servant. That very day they would climb up to the church,

Venite adoremus

robed with candles in hand they would follow the Redeemer born two days before, He Who, dressed in diamonds, would be carried in solemn procession by a crowd of children, on that day of innocence of an unhappy year, the day of Saint Stephen, December 26, 1942.

Thirty-five years before, when Checco was ready to enter the order of Saint Francis, the then-young Prince had said to his country servant: "Stay with me, we will live like Franciscans." And Checco obeyed.

THE
INFANT
JESUS

AT THE APEX of a hill covered with monuments, and far from any residential district, the church of Ara Coeli is surrounded on two sides by titans. The first stands on a square which partakes of that absolute which Renaissance beauty can attain (more than anything else, the Capitol Plaza contains the unfathomable secret of the Renaissance); the second has been in disgrace for fifty years, and is still so, but one never knows with architecture: it challenges centuries, stubborn and saucy. The stairway that leads to the church is the steepest (one hundred and twenty-four steps of white marble, and extraordinarily high and dangerously smooth, lead from the bottom of Capitol Hill to the Franciscan church

13

of Ara Coeli—watch your step when it's wet), the most uncomfortable, the most tiring in history; a sublime flight of imagination, its conquest is a point of honor to adults, a desired victory to children.

The Infant Jesus, born in the hay of a stable two nights before, now crowned King and covered with diamonds, waits for the children of Rome: it is the holiday of innocence.

The smaller ones hitch up their knees with their hands at every riser, which reaches more than half-way above their legs; at each step they give a sigh of relief. They turn around to evaluate their strength and courage, and this gives them new energy; they repress a smile on their fiery faces, which burn brighter as they move gradually upward.

Whoever goes up to the church on any other day must be a person who is willing and able to think; nobody happens to be there because of curiosity: laziness selects.

In a magnificent atmosphere, under a ceiling which compels you to stand with nose up and mouth open, you can attend a Mass read to four or five persons in the humble fashion of the Franciscans, a humility scented of roses. Such a large world will converge upon you that it will be weightless, the air as light as on a mountain peak.

On the day of Saint Stephen that stern and solitary church, where one can hear an insect's flight, becomes the most confusing and noisy, a center of cheerfulness. It is filled to overflowing with a crowd of children. They go up and down the unlikely stairway creating on it the pleasant chaos of blossoming life. There is no semblance of order, no attempt at discipline; they enter holding the string of a balloon or clenching greedily a toy found under a tree on the Eve. These are things which the Infant Jesus himself, who is entrusted with the protection of Rome, likes as much as they do; it is right that he should see them too, they want him to see, that's why they bring them.

Nor is it unusual to see a young mother covering her breast with a handkerchief, as she feeds her baby. The order springs from spontaneity and happiness. The fathers' task is to lift the small fry so that they may see in the crowd, so they can satisfy their legitimate curiosity: the ass and the ox, Saint Joseph and the Virgin; but above all the Infant Jesus in the straw crib, chubby and pink as they themselves are, crowned and dressed as King.

One thing, another, one more still. How many "But how's" and "Why's," how many questions leave the fresh small lips; the fathers have an answer for every one of them, with the utmost simplicity: father, child, and Infant Jesus are one and the same.

In front of the *crèche* stands a diminutive pulpit, which the children climb in order to recite from it Christmas poems; the Infant Jesus, bearing a king's crown and dressed with diamonds, leans out of his straw crib to listen.

The girls perform successfully one after the other, telling poems readily and often with admirable and admired ease, sometimes artificial and excessive; only infrequently does one fail the task. Some of them wait mysteriously with sealed lips before beginning, counting the audience, and they do not begin if the number is not satisfactory. Woman is a born actress. For boys it's hard, it's something else again. They have to conquer themselves before opening their mouths, and often they don't succeed; they are left overcome without having uttered a word, the audience paralyzes their voice and memory, and several as soon as they reach the pulpit even refuse to climb its steps. The tongue that within the home walls wounds ear and brains, vaults roofs, confronted with listening strangers becomes lost. Nor do promptings and supplications help; the encouragement of friends and family only makes matters worse. The diminutive orator cowers dumb and frightened, clouds over, backs away hard and inimical, ends up by fleeing; or he ends the adventure by breaking down in tears. One would say that shyness is more a male than a female quality. That's why feminine shyness is so much praised: because it is so rare.

Followed by parents, friends and relatives, children climb the forbidding stairs. From the working-class districts of the town they come in platoons, led by the strongest or biggest one, whose display of protection and authority, on the way and inside the church, anticipates fatherly richness.

Venite adoremus

God made himself into a child to reach them, without their noticing how it happened.

Venite adoremus

The adults do not shrink away from hardship on that day; they feel involved just as the children, an involvement they reaffirm and renew each year with more conscious satisfaction, if not without a vague uneasiness. As long as they can they will attempt to make it up there, even though what once had been a conquest may become a sentence.

Venite adoremus

At three o'clock that afternoon, His Excellency, the Prince of Santo Stefano also climbs, among children of his street and of all the streets of Rome, with scholarly rhythm, the Capitol Hill. Checco follows at his heels, lifting one leg at a time in the way the children do. Lost in the swarming crowd, one behind the other in Franciscan robes, with lighted candles, behind the line of children, master and servant are different only in size.

Venite adoremus

On the day of innocence and humanity.

SISTER
GIOVANNA
FRANCESCA

T HE MOTHERABBESS," said Checco, thrusting a slice of his face through His Excellency's door, after the Mother Abbess had been waiting for a short time at the threshold. Her passage across the throne room had been like a puff of air, a gust of wind, the body hardly grazing the floors; and Checco's toddling only made its speed increase.

His Excellency rose hastily to meet her, and with the movements of a crane bowed down to kiss her hand.

Twenty-five years before, his first-born daughter, Princess Maria Adelaide, had become Sister Giovanna Francesca upon entering a convent of which she was now the abbess.

Tall and thin, her pale face emerged strong-willed from

cloistral bands of unrepressed elegance. All feeling of human matter had been extinguished from it. The same effect would be had looking at her face if it had been made of wood or cardboard. Her large black eyes revealed a ceaseless activity of thought, and only an act of indulgence would bring the far memory of a smile to her lips. The long and waxen hands, exquisite, revealed the quality of her origins.

Whenever the daughter arrived alone and unexpected it was to talk about pressing or extraordinary things; but in twenty-five years her visits to her father had never been of such importance and seriousness.

For two years now Rome had been involved in a war of fortune that the people carried on without belief and enthusiasm, looking for any excuse to put it out of their minds. If it hadn't been for the darkness in which the city was kept at night, up to that moment one wouldn't have known that a war was on, notwithstanding the streets overflowing with unarmed soldiers, who seemed to be kept as extras for a comic play. Something in the machinery produced this feeling of unease, of skepticism and hopelessness that nothing could dissipate, and that became heavier by the hour. The leaders themselves had lost faith in success, and their too well-colored words fell like soap bubbles on the crowd.

A resolution of such feelings was fast approaching, and not to think about it was held by the majority to be the best attitude. An Allied landing was expected in Sicily. Its repercussions would be heard in every corner of Italy and Europe. They would produce consequences which couldn't be assessed by the imagination; the road was open to the unknown: if the state of false quiet were to be overturned, from then on the real war would begin.

"The Holy Father has given the bishops orders to be ready to face any event with Christian spirit."

18

Having said so, the Mother Abbess folded her long hands in her lap. Of the two black figures sitting one in front of the other in the darkened room, only the white of hands and paleness of faces were well defined, as in some ancient paintings where figures in mourning loom over a background of sad majesty.

His Excellency, head slightly inclined, kept silence while his daughter spoke.

"Father mine."

"Dearest daughter."

Barely lifting his head, the Prince regained his natural stature.

"Our physical person does not exist. We have silenced its material strength for a much greater conquest; for us it has no voice. Such voice must not make itself heard for any human purpose, even the most natural. It would be terrible if at the hour of suffering it should arise from its ashes. In one instant the slow and steadfast construction of our whole life would cave in. In this frail body that the Lord has given us lives a captive strength; a different, imperishable person built up day by day from the extinction of that matter, and which is now beyond our pertinence, which we cannot even evaluate and can hardly notice; nor do we realize how much it can do, for it will act by itself, it will arise like a flame. A mighty will rules over it. Even if we wanted to spare ourselves we couldn't; our actions do not belong to our frail body, nor are they led by it, but by this strength which it harbors and by which it abides, which we feel burning within for the complete extinction of the frail matter. At that point there is light: the truth."

He paused, holding high his head, then bent it slightly, lowering his voice to a familiar tone.

"If that which is coming shall be a harsh challenge to our physical person we will not feel its weight or severity, and the

19

harder it shall be the less we will. You will see what treasures will come to light without our knowing it, you will see what surprises, as if we were but spectators of ourselves, surprises that go beyond human forecast or even the possibilities of imagination. They will spring forth from us unnoticed, as leaves do from trees in spring."

The old man's voice forming these warm words stayed cold; it was obvious that nothing could happen to cast a shadow over his luminous certitude.

"Father mine."

"Dearest daughter."

The black figures arose together, facing each other. On the left that of the father, taller, on the right that of his daughter. They crossed the throne room slowly and in silence to permit their thoughts to continue the conversation. The pontifical crests and the regal chair cast rays into the darkness.

On reaching the door, the Prince bowed to kiss the hand of the Abbess with his usual crane-like movement.

Hobbling on flat feet to denounce his own lateness, Checco neared to close the door.

"See you soon, Motherabbess."

"Good-bye, Checco." The Abbess exhaled gently as she turned toward him. For the old servant she had kept in her voice unconsciously an echo of worldliness.

1943

FOR THREE YEARS Rome had
been living its nights in darkness. For three years its citizens
heard the air-raid warning sirens scream at shorter and shorter
intervals.

After a while, if the warning was given during the day,
cautious people would instinctively approach the walls of buildings as one does when it's raining to avoid getting wet; nobody
stopped on his way, and most people paid less attention to that
scream emptied of fear than they did to the noon-hour siren,
which makes one look at his watch to see if it's correct, and
makes one think of the table where steaming spaghetti or fet-
tuccine will be ready waiting.

Only those without anything else to do went down to the shelters to look for busyness, and with them went those who had made a hobby of it: the habitués, few in number but worthy of mention. There isn't a thing in the world, no matter how horrible or repulsive or that such may seem, which is without its cultists and fanatically dedicated lovers; these went below surface as professors go to their lectures or scientists to their laboratories, showing off knowledge and art, to enrich themselves daily with new theories to be passed on: victories and defeats, discoveries; in this fashion they built living novels. And hysterical women. They did as dogs do when fireworks are being shot; at the first bursts they begin to run without knowing where, how, and why, and they end up by crawling under a bed. They were not beyond dashing over the streets in nightgowns, looking like ghosts in the darkness. Thirty years of practice wouldn't have been enough to quiet them down; on the contrary, as the wisdom of the cultists grew richer each day with new information, so the unreasonable fury of the women increased each time.

If the warning was given at night the men wouldn't hear it any longer, and if in the comfort of sleep they were awakened by their more sensible and lighter-sleeping wives, they only grunted "Oh?" and, turning on their other side, returned to sleep.

This healthy composure, typical of our lucky city, ended by soothing the remnant of fear in the wives, who, after remaining for a while breathlessly straining their ears, fell asleep reassured.

On the morning of July 19, 1943, at about eleven o'clock in the morning, a number of small silvery butterflies appeared in the burning light of the Roman sky, at an incredible height. Never were butterflies seen at such altitudes, they were so small; the sirens screamed on every side as if they had lost their mind, with an insistence in their voice that could not be explained.

The small brilliant insects approached in swarms with an encircling movement that provoked unbelieving wonder. They performed in the air the figures of a ballet with grace, elegance, and precision; they appeared and disappeared in a blinding light that seemed to melt them. Not even the first crashes that the Romans were hearing after three years of war, full of the sinister noise of illegitimate death, could jolt the certainty rooted in their heart.

In the center of town people stood in the squares and on the streets with their noses to the sky, smilingly satisfying a naive and unknowing curiosity, and almost admiration, for such a novel and fetching show. The more fearful ones caught outdoors by the bombing sought refuge behind the doors of buildings kept barely open by doorkeepers who wanted to close, and there they stayed whispering together, sticking their heads out once in a while waiting for the good weather. The insistent circling of the little silver beasts, now more and more visible and shining, and the regular repetition of crashes that violated the air which had grown to a body of unknown density—in places barely audible because of the absorbing effect of the hills on which the city is built—informed even the most remote and skeptical that the railroad station was being bombed.

From eleven to one o'clock: exactly two hours.

Two hours were enough to alter the face of Rome. You could have seen in those two hours the smiles disappear, one by one, from all lips. And the air itself, brimming with peace, was changed in two hours.

When the sirens signaled the end of the raid, at about two o'clock, everyone's first thought was of getting news, since nobody had even an approximate idea of what had happened.

23

The phones had undergone a pathological crisis; those of the bombed districts didn't answer.

The early news was dismal, and after each minute it grew worse.

Not satisfied with what could be learned, many rushed to the station in feverish haste.

The Termini station, with its congenial nineteenth-century front, showed no sign of disturbance: it was intact, the air around so quiet and sweetly drowsy in the still heat of the summer afternoon, that it seemed there to allay any fear. But such calm could not overcome suspicion and fear; the contrast made them only more ominous. The bombs had hit a few hundred yards behind, along the rail lines. At Santa Bibiana, as if a curtain had been raised over a stage, the impact of the disaster was shown in all its crudeness: San Lorenzo, the teeming district flanking the railroad, was agonizing in its utter desolation.

Broken mains were causing floods everywhere, gas pipes made the air in some places unbreatheable. Many houses had crumbled: hills of rubbish. Others were only partially ruined; gutted, their entrails swung from walls still standing: furniture, mattresses, sheets, carpets, blankets. Still others were seriously endangered; plowed by huge gashes, they were ready to fall any minute. Some that had been built especially well kept their internal walls while the front fell clear off; one could see rooms perfectly arranged, conjugal beds made up with sparkling sheets turned lovingly over the blankets, and the image of the Virgin watching over a happy marriage. A small table with a radio and, surviving at a now unreachable height on the windowsill, a vase of geraniums and a caged canary, an unknowing and innocent victim who unfurled his song, putting into it all he had in order to be heard from such height and in such confusion. Many houses had only the outside walls

24

standing, they seemed unharmed; inside was a void, everything overwhelmed and swallowed by the abyss.

Because of the time at which the bombing occurred, men were at work and many women were shopping; at home had stayed mainly the old and very young—a great number of children were home because of the vacations—and they were slaughtered.

Their fathers, hurrying with picks and shovels, dug in the carnage affecting a hope which they would not confide even to themselves, with a strenuousness that revealed the need for some activity which could absorb their whole consciousness. So many children, the same who had climbed the stairway to the Ara Coeli on the day of Saint Stephen with flaming cheeks, to visit the Infant Jesus and recite poems to Him. Beautiful and happy children of Rome, so desired, so loved, born in happiness and for it, they closed a just-begun existence in a vision of Hell.

In two hours Rome lost 10,500 of her sons.

From many directions came wails and shouts of those still living and buried under the ruins, conveying less the depth of their pain than the abasement of their powerlessness, the cruelty of not being able to do anything. And suddenly one could see something moving in the dust, a thing of mud and ashes among mud and ashes, a thing aquiring human outlines, eyes throwing darts whose appeal, like that of the voices which came from underground, could be resisted only with great efforts. Someone succeeded in opening a passage in the rubbish and seeing light again. He dragged his body like a reptile towards the others, without strength to stand erect in returning from death; the face and eyes covered with mud expressed the possibility that so much happiness might be another greater danger for his mind. Some store signs were left standing at the foot of collapsed houses: Wine, Barber, Novelties. . . . And

loyally and bravely backed out acknowledging to have lost was considered a traitor.

After a heroic but too weak resistance, Rome fell in the hands of those who formerly were allies, now occupying foes.

Patrols crossed and re-crossed the streets of the capital. Trucks loaded with soldiers, sub-machine guns leveled, roamed in every direction. The season for hunting men was opened: scapegoats were needed for a responsibility which hunched their shoulders; they had to kill in order to give vent to disillusion, to desperation, give vent to bestial rage and cruelty. There was need to jail, deport, kill; to kill for the sake of killing, any pretext was good to kill. The most painful thing is that Italians helped, and sometimes led, the new enemy in his quest. On this we can only defer conclusions; we do not feel so superior that we may claim a right to pass judgment.

As soon as the city was placed under military rule, the Prince of Santo Stefano gave orders to lock the palace gate and keep unfastened the hatch for entering and leaving. Via Monserrato, with its big doors shut to a crack or half-opened, took on a mourning air as if death had been in all the houses.

One night Bice went up panting to the master: two women had taken shelter in her porter's room, one old and one younger with three children; they were asking to talk with the Prince.

"We are Jewish, they are looking for us, they have taken away our men. There is nowhere we can hide, we are poor, we must save the children; we have promised it to our men, who went to die."

Opening the door wide, the Prince gave orders to let them come up immediately. The women climbed the staircase in misery. One of the children was held in his mother's arms. His Excellency and Checco took the mattresses off their beds and carried them to the large hall, where the women spread them at the foot of the papal throne, which in the flickering

28

light of a candle assumed an unreal stateliness. Bice also brought a mattress, while Checco went into his closet to find a blanket. Even a few pieces of bread were uncovered, and for the children a drink of milk. Bice took care of that.

The Jewish women had an expression in which pain had surrendered to fatalism, they did not seem to suffer. The children looked ill because of the confusion they couldn't understand; only the one in his mother's arms fell asleep peacefully.

Before going to rest the Prince talked to the women hunched in a corner, eyes shining from perplexed faces. "Be reassured, don't worry, sleep without fear; your children will be saved and you with them. Nobody will find you, no one will uncover your trail; those who live in this house will not betray you, and I am here to help, to defend you. We will prepare better and more permanent quarters as soon as we can. The Lord watches over you, sleep in peace."

The Prince and his valet retired to rest, and before leaving him, His Excellency told Checco: "Tomorrow after Mass you'll go to Norina's and ask to speak with her in my name. Tell her we have fugitives at home and we don't know how to nourish them. Meanwhile I shall go to talk to the Mother Abbess."

In the morning they arose before dawn, and when they left Santa Lucia they separated as always and hurried on opposite ways. When they returned home, they reassured the women lying on their bedding in oriental posture, whose life had taken refuge entirely in their eyes. They had words of courage and comfort for their safety and health. In fact in less than two hours packages of food began to arrive, full of supplies for the adults and children, and among them delicacies and tidbits which succeeded in illuminating those lead-gray faces. Norina never let a need go unfulfilled.

Next evening two young and two older Jewish women knocked

at Bice's door. Hunting Jews had become the foremost goal of the enemy; the hunt was especially focused on the district next to ours, between Torre Argentina and the Tiber.

The throne room was the only space which the Prince could apportion. The wretched women were let in, while more aid was being sent from several places. Sacks, rags, blankets . . . . In the afternoon the Abbess arrived. She descended with her wings in the middle of the hall, a soaring figure next to which that of her father had become a tower.

"For the two women and the children I have already made arrangements." She breathed the words like a soft wind in the heavy atmosphere of the room. "Tomorrow a car with a Vatican plate will come for them." And turning toward the others: "Soon you will all be safe, do not be afraid; men we cannot accommodate but if there are any we will take care of them too. If we cannot keep you together now, it is in order that later you can be more safely reunited. You will have news of each other, do not fear anything." And as the words skimmed over their heads, the Abbess was seen disappearing in the same fashion as she had come; the air was her natural environment.

Other Jewish women knocked at the door, always with infants, children and youths; it was opened also to men: the door opened for all who knocked.

The Abbess sometimes called twice a day, and from Norina's house larger parcels arrived daily.

Encamped in that unusual room, around a throne and on its step, there were as many as twenty-nine Jews at one time waiting to be settled in safe places.

And when Checco's long ears caught the rumor that someone in the district took pains to repeat that the Santo Stefano palace had become a branch of the Synagogue, the Prince was seen coming down the stairs carrying a sign, followed by Checco with a ladder. Out in the street Checco propped the ladder against the door, and the Prince climbed it with quick and sure steps. Under the coat of arms he hung the sign; on it was written in large characters: "Holy See."

1 9 4 4

IT WAS A mournful winter, that of 1944, when the springs of joy seemed to have run dry.

Piazza Navona remained mute and deserted for the days of Christmas and Twelfth-Night. Missing on that night devoted to children were the boisterous stalls of toys—one doesn't know whether fathers or children find them more amusing. In an outburst of carefree candor, the adults propose to celebrate with them and for their sake the inextinguishable youthfulness of life, and in the perfect hour they forget its weight and worries. In friendship they forget rivalry. Not a sign of merrymaking now among the majestic walls, used to house all that festivity.

As far as memory went, never had the joyous city been so sad. The echo of those happy hours seemed also to have faded, as if they could not be revived even in memory.

German patrols were roaming the streets night and day, and trucks loaded with armed militia crossed them over and again to maintain what remained of the laws, which, being arbitrary, constituted for others the height of illegality. The ability to evade their grasp or to founder into it depended on good or ill chance, shrewdness, and acrobatics worthy of the jungle. The reasons for hate fed on each other and multiplied; at each new discovery a shout of bitter satisfaction and gruesome jubilation arose as the misunderstanding went on growing in the way of an avalanche. Everyone felt a gun pointing at his back, like wildlife in the forest when the season opens. Unable to judge objectively, to heed a selfless impulse which could have cleared the misunderstanding, under the yoke of defeat which aggravated their wretchedness, they had become enraged against those who by the very fact that they were alive condemned error and wrongdoing. In order for the first to be right, the others had to be killed to the last man.

The citizen who from inside his home heard hobnailed steps resound ominously in the emptiness of the street suffered minutes of unbearable anguish, felt a need to clutch his head, which reason seemed to have abandoned.

How can so many causes of hate and vengeance stockpile over mankind's head? Why can't they be resolved for the common good and to mutual advantage? Why is it impossible to free the human species from the webs of this damned net in which it's bound? What is this curse which makes us hate and destroy each other, and defile the gift of life?

These were questions that a citizen who wasn't poisoned by hate asked himself, clutching his head in his hands at the hour of anguish.

33

People flocked to the churches in prayer. It was the only place where one could find relief, recover some instants of peace. A peace once so well rooted into the soul, yet so quickly and completely lost. It was the only place where a spot of light was left. To pray meant that one could enter that light, open one's heart to hope; to hope meant to believe in something, in salvation; to believe in salvation meant that it could be achieved.

Towards the end of February Rome heard the voice of the guns that were to resolve the tragic state into which it had fallen. The Allied armies had established a bridgehead near the harbor of Anzio, and from there planned to reach the city. That voice became friendly, ruling the endless days of waiting, the long nights of vigil. Following the voice which rose and fell as the light of a candle, hope and despair rose and fell in one's heart. We groped expecting some good of guns, hoped for salvation through them, as does the sick man who, not being able to endure pain any longer, calls for death.

March 24 was cold and gray, of a rawness almost unknown in Rome. Low clouds, from which only a few icy drops were allowed to fall by a stinging wind, rolled through the afternoon.

In St. Peter's Square a dark and sparse crowd was gathering, huddled as if against the cold, towards the gates of the church where the prelates of the chapter chanted psalms in that voice which transforms the senses of the listener into loudspeakers. The crowd moved closer because of the cold, and the increasing wind pushed the clouds down to the ground. The crowd pressed forward towards the front, on which a door to a balcony suddenly opened, and unexpectedly the Pope stepped out. He was without his court, without his following; only two prelates were at his side, and they seemed to decrease in size as if they wanted to disappear: his stature became ever taller. The violence of the wind swept the red cape over his head and as soon as he began talking the words were snatched from his mouth and scattered under the low clouds between the sky and the ground.

Nobody had ever seen Pius XII so much alone, so unadorned. And as he went on with his very short speech, every word standing by itself, detached, he seemed taller and more lonely.

He spoke to a crowd very different from the usual one that on radiant days slowly fills, like clear waters, the whole square of Saint Peter's. Now the square was still mostly empty. The people had come for an emergency, crowding before the church because of the cold that paralyzed their bones, shivering with fever; they crowded there as a sick child would seek shelter at his mother's breast, knowing without having to be told that there isn't a warmer and more secure refuge in the whole world. The words of the Pope—incisive, cutting—pierced those shivers to the bones. Above all fears, respect or convention, with the wide, assured gestures of an arm that seemed of superhuman length, he appeared to be flinging far away and with extreme violence an anathema. Pius XII from his balcony called out a clear warning to the two armies who were fighting for the city at its gates.

Rome was not to be touched, and woe onto whomever dared to touch it.

The passion propelled the voice high and far; it seemed to battle with the clouds between Heaven and earth. It was so unexpected: nobody would have believed the Pope of human sweetness, always ready to smile and to caress, the correct diplomat, to be capable of such violence. From that balcony in the cold wind of the sad March day, through the mouth of a man the wrath of God was heard. The crowd moved closer together, merging benumbed. After a short blessing the Pope disappeared and the large window again closed mercilessly on the cold.

And then spring came with all its warm spells, its flirting incantations, its deceits, its innocent cruelty; the Romans were frustrated because they couldn't respond, like someone ill who from behind the windowpane can see life go on as usual, ignoring his pain.

Surrounded by useless and incomprehensible hatred, the population flooded the churches. Women stayed for long periods, each hunched in her grief of mother or wife. Men, those who had stayed and who had the courage to walk in the besieged city, stood erect, silent, as if waiting for an answer to an implicit question. Their stillness was even more moving.

It came to be known that the statue of the Virgin of Divine Love had left her sanctuary between Rome and the sea and, like other refugees, was hidden in town. The Roman people, who was used to making spring pilgrimages to the sanctuary, pilgrimages that became more numerous as the month of May advanced, seemed to look for her, to guess her breathing, to perceive the rustle of her robes. Where did the Virgin hide, the one elected by the Romans as the spiritual mother of their town, the mother of Roman mothers?

One day towards the end of May, when her absence was most deeply felt, while the voice of the guns was heard to increase in violence from the sea, the Virgin of Divine Love appeared from nowhere on the altar of the Church of St. Ignatius, in the center of town.

Like swarms of robins the Romans converged on St. Ignatius, a crowd that on the last days of May increased out of all proportions. Prayers were held even at night, and organized groups of citizens kept watch. It lasted for two weeks without any interruption, like the thaw of a river that floods its banks and conquers everything. At the end of this period the people witnessed an extraordinary sight: the former allied army, which for nine months had kept the city under its heel, cruelly exercising its unearned power, was silently filing across the streets, disturbed by the sound of its own iron-shod steps, weapons at the ready. From one end of the city to the other, exhausted and ill-equipped soldiers streamed by on improvised conveyances that in different circumstances would have provoked hilarious laughter. Not yet convinced of their defeat, they walked with heads hanging in a deadly tiredness that they weren't able to hide. Some viewers, too forgiving or too forgetful, expressed pity at their passage. In the meanwhile, behind them in the night arrived the soldiers who carry stars on their banner. They moved with supple bodies and velvet steps, as if afraid of waking someone. Rome was saved, unhurt. It was freed of all the intolerable misunderstandings, established in a position that was neither beautiful nor comfortable, but clear: that of the loser. Reality had to be accepted, instead of a life in that unreal world from which all infamy originates.

After his speech of March 24 the Pope had not reappeared. The Pope's presence in Rome is like that of a lamp that burns unseen, whose rare appearances are an occasion for all to give thanks for the warmth that always radiates from it.

June the 6th, in the afternoon resplendent with sun, the tall, white, fleshless body appeared on the balcony of St. Peter's surrounded by high prelates in magnificent robes of the utmost pomp—scarlet, purple, indigo, draped with intricate embroideries and golden chains, crosses of gems—surrounded by dignitaries and heads of knightly orders, by foreign diplomats, who formed a crown around the Pope as members of a large family. This time too the Pope said only a few words, but so different in that light of vespers from those uttered the stormy day two months before: his soul seemed drained of all bitterness. On the square were cars of all kinds, peaceful and warlike, covered with groups of American soldiers. On their serene, youthful faces joy assumed a virginal expression. And the Romans feasted with them, receiving in answer flowers and packs of cigarettes; it seemed that a victory was being celebrated, the brightest and most complete victory. One has to know how to take events, and Rome does it with practiced experience. There was no double meaning in that behavior, no expedient, malice; it was an instant of abandon, of spontaneous and sincere happiness which enabled the people to forget things that a few hours earlier had clawed deep gashes in the soul and that now seemed far away and remote, removed to the museum of the past.

Rome was saved: unharmed.

And as from that festive tide shouts of gratitude began to rise towards the Pope, as if the miracle had come from the strength of his position or the prestige of his person, he left the Vatican to unburden the weight he felt piling on his conscience. Like one who shakes the dust from his clothes he left the Vatican—an unheard-of event—as any citizen would have done, he left his home for St. Ignatius to kneel and give thanks to the Virgin of Divine Love. The miracle had not been his work; it was not due to his person, but to his faith. The miracle consisted in having believed in salvation, and he who had been the first to believe was the first to give thanks; the miracle was to have anchored oneself to a point from which everything could be expected, even the salvation of Rome.

BILLY-BET

ON HEARING these syllables in Roman or continental society, one would not have thought that they referred to people who spent a more or less normal existence—the two names merged to form something unique, exceptional, extraordinary; similar to flowers that mysteriously, and so effortlessly, diffuse scent and color through the air.

Prince Guglielmo Sucarelli of Naples and the Roman Princess Elisabetta di Santo Stefano had in marrying achieved the ultimate and seldom reached goal of marriage: to make of two one person, and even one name. It could have occurred to no one to utter Bet without Billy or Billy without Bet. Their union was so perfect, absolute, attained with such ease, without having done anything to bring it about; even more, without knowing of having achieved it, as if it were the easiest and most accessible thing to anyone.

They belonged to two rich families that the events had slowly converted to poverty; first class nobility, ancient and authentic. Billy was left with the barely visible remains of his ancestral fortunes, a few crumbs, to which was added at the beginning a small replenishment by the usual aunt, who on her deathbed had shown the last definitive weakness for her favorite nephew, happy to do for his sake, on leaving for the skyward flight, one more injustice. Bet was given by her father a dowry which was completely inadequate to the name she carried and her style of life. The Prince of Santo Stefano had given all he could, wringing himself dry for his second daughter, who was marrying a poor nobleman. A brave and useless effort, bordering on the ridiculous.

Billy-Bet had lived together for almost twenty years and were now straddling the fourth decade. They were tall and handsome, with a sure and refined elegance obviously inborn; both had been dark-haired at birth, but the Princess had dyed her hair blonde, extremely blonde, like Venus and Isolde, incredibly blonde. They both spoke four languages with perfect accuracy and confidence, with excellent accent; they both were lucky and able gamblers: the game was their track. Their background was so solid, so permanent, that they did not remember its existence, as they did not remember their poverty. They had never owned a house but they owned a car, custom-made, superb, which they exchanged following the fashions, the latest cry; it was their earthly base and only possession, and both drove it equally well and alternately. Great hotels sheltered them, the ones whose names conjure fairy tales in the mind; they lived in them as if at home, and moved following the seasons as swallows do, toward the places where at any given time the warmth of life throbbed strongest, where life boiled most fervently. Billy-Bet: at these syllables, which in those circles had become a respected and undisputed brand-name, every door would open. Poor as they were, their life was of the most expensive, among people who were famous for their riches, among people from every part of the world who were fabulously, relentlessly, scandalously rich.

They had had no children and they had never desired or even thought about having them, almost as if they did not know what happens when men and women come together; if children had been born they would have taken them with the same simplicity, a most natural thing, nor did they suffer even in thought from regretting their absence. For almost twenty years they had been doing, unruffled and undisturbed, what seems to most people impossible, unattainable, absurd: without owning a cent they spent money in unlimited amounts, without any care; what's more, they showed in spending unlimited imagination. Richness was due to a couple of such true ancestry, so handsome, cheerful, elegant; the rich catered to them, especially the new ones, those not yet refined, the ones whose wealth originated from obscure sources, the ones too much talked about. Unfathomable mysteries of this inexhaustible life.

As she jumped from the car with the lightness of a doe, and as her foot entered the dark portal of the parental house, the voice of Princess Elisabeth, high and harmonious, silvery, echoed from the walls, "Bice! Bice! Bice!" And, expanding to the ceiling with a smiling momentum, it seemed to overwhelm the rigid walls until it filled the whole house; "Bice! Bice! Bice!" she shouted to the gatekeeper who had appeared on the threshold of her cubicle and, black in her clerical robe, kept bowing low to the twice Princess. Her husband followed with a golden laughter of his whole body: "What is our Bice up to?" Laughter filled with the potentialities of an orchestra. "Checco!

41

Checco! Checco!" cried the Princess on reaching the top of the stairs: "How are you, Checco?" And the consort at her side: "What is our Checco up to?"

Crossing the throne hall she talked to her husband in a high, slightly ostentatious voice, afraid perhaps of being overcome by the air and by the cold that the place inspired, while the husband came to her aid with an effective display of the whole range of his laughs. Checco followed them, not entirely convinced of the necessity of speeding up his duck-walk. Unconsciously, they felt the power of that darkness at the same time that their voices brought violence to it. They were forcing its light and its air, the color of things and its eternal immobility, as if fireworks had been shot in those austere shadows.

The Prince was standing in the middle of the room, and as soon as Bet entered the door, without a movement toward her, he opened his arms, receiving his daughter who threw herself running into them.

"Daddy! Daddy! Daddy!"

Disengaging himself from the daughter's embrace, the Prince turned to his son-in-law who, taking the proferred hand and bowing with deep devotion, touched it with his lips.

Bending toward them imperceptibly, the old man told Billy-Bet to sit down on the small sofa in front of him.

"We are coming from Lisbon, Daddy, we arrived yesterday morning, this is our first visit." The father nodded his head in acknowledgment. "We passed by Gibraltar and we stopped in Tangiers for a few days, how nice it was! What a good time! So many people we know! Half of Europe was there." The old man did not show signs of pleasure at his daughter's glad news; they did not produce any more effect on him than outside noises on the ramparts of a fortress.

"But what we saw on our return to Italy, the things we had to see passing through Naples and on our drive here, it's all one big wreck, ruin after ruin, it takes away your breath, a nightmare. As soon as one enters Rome one seems to return into the world, one can breathe at last. How could all this have happened?"

"Daughter, dear," answered the father without surrendering a degree of his composure, "when certain things have happened it is perfectly useless to find out their causes, to establish who is more and who is less responsible for them, to whom their legitimate paternity belongs. For the moment there are better and more important things to do; we have to repair all these damages in the best and shortest possible way."

"All this happened during the nine months we were away."

"Indeed," answered the old man. Then, in order to soften the abruptness of his answer, he added: "You see how a short time is enough to change so many things."

"Have you suffered much?" Bet wanted to follow on his tack. Billy for the moment kept quiet; it was hard for him to start the show with his repertoire, he could not find the appropriate cue.

"No material or physical sufferings could equal the awful moral one, at the sight of mankind lost, blinded by a hate that had become a principle and an end in itself."

"And Rome, as usual, made it by the skin of its teeth," chimed in Billy with a loud laugh, and Bet giggled in support. To pause at this point would have been to leave a void; like an air-pocket for a plane, it would have meant a dangerous loss of altitude, an unforgivable tactical error for someone so sophisticated.

"And this is what you call making it by the skin of the teeth? Our hearts are blighted, scarred: this is the truth. The walls of Rome are undamaged."

"Rome will always pull through."

"If the Lord has wished to show mercy for His city, this

should only recall us to our duties; He did it to let us feel the greatness of His love for us, but at the same time to make us feel how large our debt and how serious our tasks are. It would be a curse not to realize this, to misunderstand; to hold back, for us, is unforgivable; the most devastating punishment would fall on these walls that have this time been spared."

The inspired quiet with which the old man uttered his words made the two of them unbearably uncomfortable, so that Bet felt the urgent need to descend to a confidential tone.

"Did the Germans really become that nasty at the end?"

"When the beast is set free inside the man, the more and less do not matter; everything is of the same quality."

"Last time we were in Rome we left the Excelsior full of Germans, it was just like being in Germany, it did not seem possible they could do such things; they seemed such nice boys. Billy, do you remember how dear they were! They must have turned about all at once. Remember Fritz? Otto? Franz? Oskar? The darlings, we used to play together all night long."

"Men are not exactly created by geometricians with their rulers; those who are darlings at one time can be very different at another."

"You know what it is? They are obedient without any reservations, they aren't like us who, when they tell us to go one way, feel right away like going in the opposite direction; they obey blindly, without thinking, full speed ahead. You can imagine what happens when their choice falls on a leader who is criminal or crazy. Now the Excelsior is full of Americans; such pleasant big children, it's a delight, we are playing all night, it's like being in America."

The darkening air became heavier, like a blanket that threatens to take away your breath; nobody thought of lighting a lamp, which was anyway nowhere to be seen. Even if the very small light at the foot of the old ivory crucifix had been turned

44

on, and the other, microscopic, on the stand next to the Prince's bed, together they would not have solved the problem; rather, they would have only made it worse.

The two of them glared at the old man's shape, which was becoming more and more black, bringing out in contrast the paleness of the hands and of the face; they felt on the verge of being submerged with all their baggage of neat exclamations and giggles in an unalterable shipwreck. Trying to avoid it, Bet looked for her husband's face:

"You know, Billy, Daddy is like the flowers that one takes to the shrine on Good Thursdays; remember, Daddy, how beautiful they were, and they are all white because they let them grow in the darkness, they are like those beautiful wigs of the eighteenth century; remember, Daddy, when you and we children used to plant them and take the pots down to the cellar?"

But no matter what they could say or do, they were getting lost in those shadows that overcame any possibility of reaction.

Almost as if by magic, Checco entered from the little side door, and without a word went with his horizontal steps to the desk under the window to light an invisible lamp. Never did he take so long to cross that room. The guests followed his movements in silence, as those of a ghost; and when the bulb was lit, Billy burst out with such a spontaneous laugh, so sincere and out of place, the likes of which he had not had as far as memory goes, and which was in no way related to the ones that he produced custom-made and in harmony from morning to night. In any other situation, this completely controlled man, in whom nature had been transformed into style, would have been able to keep it back; this time he just couldn't, it had to burst out: with the light on, the room was darker than before. To keep above water was a hopeless task. They felt themselves sinking in an obscurity beyond any resource, any reserve. Only their startled and somewhat frightened eyes roved about, growing larger by the terror of extinction, to come eventually to rest on those of the Prince, his enormous eyes, which in that lighting radiated with a sweet flame all their beauty. They looked at the old man as the man does who returns to the country and the peasants among whom he had been humbly nursed, who returns after many years and after having conquered riches, and thinks to himself, as he looks around unbelieving: "Was it really here that I sucked the milk of a woman?" Yes, it was here. It was in that dark palace from which the most tiny sign of life had been exiled, that the beautiful blonde Princess, so brilliant and elegant, so sophisticated, had been nursed and had spent her childhood. And it was here, Billy thought, that I came one day to ask for the hand of a woman full of color and life.

At this point Billy, avoiding the impoliteness of glancing at his watch—which moreover couldn't have been read in that light—said to his wife:

"Bet, the hour has come, we have only enough time to dress for dinner."

"Yes . . . we are going now," answered Bet, awakened from an unknown, unidentifiable stupor. "Daddy! Daddy! Daddy!" repeated Bet loudly once on her feet, determined to climb up the slope no matter what.

Crossing the immense dark hall, lighted very weakly through the open door of the Prince's room, they both turned instinctively towards the throne which, in that light, had increased in size frighteningly, and felt pursued by its shadow.

"Checco! Checco! Checco! Bye now, bye Checco!"

What exactly Checco could have answered as he went to close the door is not known; he mumbled some words, he seemed to be angry with someone, so he was taking it out on himself.

"Our Checco."

And at the bottom of the stairs where, because of the war restrictions on lighting, one had to find one's way by touch, the

Princess took up her shouting again from her husband's side, who in his turn took up his laughs, as usual.

"Bice! Bice! Bice! Bye now, bye Bice!" she repeated until she reached the gate and, without seeing the summoned person, jumped into the car with the lightness of a doe—

"Bye darling, bye now, bye, Bice."

1 9 4 5

NO PEOPLE IS so wonderful-
ly created for peace as the people of Rome: the sky is transparent
light blue; from it the sun colors all things rosy, and evokes a
smile on every mouth.

The Roman was not made for drama, though no other people
can boast of a past as dramatic as his, not even the people of
Israel. He doesn't know exactly everything that has happened
in his ancient house, but he can feel the events vaguely hovering
above his head, and he breathes them in with the air. He knows
that many, many things have happened and that many, many
things will happen; he does not like to go deeper into the matter,
or make room for it in his mind. Once in a while, he gathers a

flower from it to embellish himself. Curiosity does not worm its way inside him, and surely not morbid curiosity; he likes to enlarge things that are beautiful and comfortable, not the ones that are ugly and hard. To the former he adds baubles and fringes; the latter ones, if possible, are hidden away. He likes to live and is happy to exist. He isn't lazy, as they say, nor indifferent, as one may believe; yet he is never in a hurry. A rushing existence he disapproves of, he loves to taste life with serenity, and in this he is a most discriminating patrician. He does not pursue opportunities, but when he meets one he knows how to take it by the forelock. He ignores fanaticism, is never an extremist, for he thinks that fanaticism and extremism are impolite and in bad taste. The larger things are, the smaller he sees them, activating his energies and resistances. He employs the strongest effort to square his shoulders and face those hardships that are impossible to avoid with a sense of balance and good health. No form of government finds opposition in him; he accepts them readily, on principle, and from each he adopts the pleasing parts; he loves pageantry, theatrics. The pageants that the Roman people can display are of inestimable beauty; therefore, he is always ready to make noise, much noise: with his mouth, his hands, because it is part of the happiness of living, and because nothing hides it as well as noise. He likes to skim the cream off his cup, never trusts its contents. He doesn't give in or retreat, his position is always on the defensive, to defend his life, his grace. To be always involved only on the surface is his salvation. When a government falls, no one excepted, he cheers even louder, this time in earnest, and only then does he reveal himself a little.

And so when one morning he was told that the man who for twenty years had governed with so much success had been shot, and hung upside down in a square of Milan, this did not seem new nor serious, but the most natural of events: "This also happens, this is also done, one can do even worse," and it's not easy to know what he feels. He closes in to save himself, for the love of life he has to save himself, has to resist, and as a defense he cheers very loudly and makes as much noise as he can.

CHECCO

Under extraordinary circumstances, Checco talked to himself. It would have been very difficult for someone interested in knowing what he was saying to gather the meaning of even one of those words. It was the muttering of a pot that because of an uncertain fire boils haphazardly, without any rule. The heat that made his lips boil, however, was the best ordered and ruled in the world. One could have counted the words that left the Prince's mouth in the course of one day, and sometimes for Checco they just weren't enough. So to satisfy himself he had to supplement them with some of his own, which he addressed to himself in the form of questions and answers. Balancing on his flat

51   139069

feet in the cubbyhole next to that of the master, which served him as kitchen and bedroom, he turned round and round without being aware of it, and went on muttering his incomprehensible questions and answers. From the next room the Prince would hear and would let him go on for a while; but if he noticed that a short outburst wasn't enough and that the exercise promised to continue for long, he would intervene:

"What is it, Checco?"

This time, too, the Prince cast the bait. His face was alien to smiles, but when it was turned to the servant with whom he had lived for forty years as a friend, the brightest of smiles was in that stern voice, and the words were like a caress from beginning to end. The Prince loved Checco's happy ignorance, which he thought to be the highest privilege that a man could have: the natural simplicity that nothing had succeeded in disturbing, and through which he could express with angelic purity an unshaken certitude that cannot be reached by the most sophisticated of men through knowledge, cannot be learned from any teachings; a certitude that blooms in a rare and favorable climate similar to the one that makes the beauty of a flower glow. He thought of him as a privileged being, an oasis of peace among the strife of passions and hatred, the fever of desires, the disorders of selfishness and rivalry; the pointless exertions of men pursuing the conquest of a handful of flies. Unresponsive to any invitation that might come from outside, to any flattery, closed to every form of corruption, Checco had remained as pure as on the day he had first seen the light. Doubt had never brushed against the serenity of that soul across which no cloud had ever passed. He had been able to keep himself so for a higher destiny, as someone who can walk through flames unharmed. For the Prince he was an example and a warning: the strongest and the most admired. A smile lingered even at night across that small round face reddened by healthy blood; it seemed to shine even stronger when he slept, as if keeping watch over his bliss. Who had taught wisdom to a being who knew nothing? He was almost illiterate, had learned to scrawl a few words as a child from the priest of his village. Every time that it came to writing on a piece of paper, "Francesco Marchetti," it had been a very troublesome enterprise; and while he wrote badly and with such difficulty, his face expressed a satisfaction the likes of which no master of the quill had ever felt. And no matter what worries troubled him, he would be anything but prompt in answering the master, who went on caressing him with his voice while waiting to see him appear.

"What's happened? What did they do to you?"

"To me they haven't done a thing, but what do those people want? Who are they sore at?"

He stopped at the door of the room waiting for an answer, hands on his waist.

"Who are those people?"

Walking through the center of Rome he had seen Colonna Square surrounded by police, while in the middle other officers mounted on trucks and riot cars were dispersing with truncheons a screaming and threatening mob.

"Who are they yelling those bad words at?"

"At no one. At their unhappiness which others exploit after having produced. Things won't be made right with curses and threats. When men have been deprived of faith and have been taught to hate work, so that they see it as an unbearable burden which provides illicit gain for crooked exploiters, then nothing is left but to go into the squares and shout the inner void which devours them, until they look like lost souls. Man reduced to a mere passage for food faces despair as soon as food becomes scarce or tasteless."

"They yell they want justice."

53

"Certainly they want justice, and they are fully entitled to it, but the justice they are shown as bait is a fraud and will not materialize. Justice will not become a reality unless helped by love, inspired and shaped by it. It is the others who have to start out and meet the poor, it is the others who must understand this human craving for justice. The world is divided into strong and weak; it always has been and always will be. The strong have always ruled and always will, the weak can only obey; they are in the others' power, at their mercy. Action must be brought against the souls of the strong; that is the battlefield on which justice should be achieved, at least as its basic needs are concerned. As long as only the weak will shout for justice, it will be so much wasted breath; they will shout forever without achieving it, they will only give sustenance to a profitable profession. Whenever a man sits at a well-laden table, he should lose his appetite at the thought of those who cannot appease their own and their children's hunger; or of those who have to make do with a piece of bread or a slice of corn meal. He ought to despise himself to the point of being unable to eat. This thought should not allow him a happy meal or a peaceful dream until he knows that all his fellowmen have enough to provide for their hunger. Nobody thinks of this when sitting down to eat; people think only about serving well their own stomachs until pleasantly and completely satisfied and agreeably filled. Yet the small flame burns at the bottom of the heart of every man who is not a brute or a criminal, kept as low as is possible — when it's so low one can pretend not to see it — but it's there because it's impossible to turn it off. It is against this lack of concern that one has to fight until persuasion is effected; against the selfishness of the strong the small flame must flare up, must illuminate the souls and give that superior happiness which no material possession can bestow. The world has always been a battlefield of violence and things haven't changed. Violence of any kind leaves things as they were; every betterment has been due to an act of reason, of patient and mature concern. Those unfortunate people shout against the ones they think or see as favored by fortune, against their masters, tyrants and oppressors; but already leading their ranks are the people who will be lucky tomorrow: the new masters, the tyrants and oppressors of tomorrow, whom they will have raised themselves and against whom they will begin to shout and fight uselessly. Only violence will silence them. The battle always rages among the strong and they use the weak as tools. No matter who wins, only the names and forms change, the situation remains the same. Things are even worse in countries where they have used violence in the hope of establishing justice or equality; distances are wider and more obvious, they are established rigidly until the time comes that a new force arises to topple them over. The social structure, which for natural reasons it is impossible to suppress, and against which it would be useless and too dangerous to rebel, is kept up by an iron hierarchy. Just as in the army, where under a draconian law there are those who order and those who obey without a chance to object. An order obtained through violence is maintained through violence. Only the guards change. The new power changes the signs and uniforms. Ease and poverty are alike everywhere; an easy life provided with every comfort and moral satisfaction on the one hand, and a hard life snatched away in unhealthy, sad places by the sweat of one's body on the other. Here at least men toil in warm sunshine, cheered by a glass of wine. Earlier they used to sing while working, and it was a pleasure to listen; now they think about justice, they think about killing someone because their work has become a thing of sadness. It is impossible for all to become rich as it is impossible for all to become doctors. To clean streets—and there will always be streets—to keep them up, to make and

55

move bricks—because houses will always be built—one doesn't have to study for twenty years.

"What is true for individuals is also true for nations. There are countries where everyone is well off, everyone has a job which allows a decent and pleasant life, and there are others where conditions are so unfavorable that some can't find enough bread. Here too it is useless to fall back on violence. Wars only produce unhappiness, destruction, death, and blind injustice. At the end both parties will be worse off than before. The world of the strong stays and grows through wars; the reaches remain wide as they were before. It doesn't help to shout in the squares, deluded by those who have an interest in feeding, exploiting and increasing unease and dissatisfaction as much as possible. That which cannot be forgiven is to take away from man the faith that develops his moral and spiritual strength, that raises him to supernatural heights; and to make him hate work, which is the measure of earthly strength, the right to a place in society, the reason and pride for living. It is not from violence that we should expect justice but from love, from this seed that man has hidden within the soul and which he too often forgets. This seed has to be watered if it is to grow and to develop. Justice conquered through violence hides evil in its origins: justice conquered with love shall be imperishable."

Checco listened, without a word or a movement, to his master's words. Never through all the years had they had such a long and important conversation. As far as its meaning was concerned, it didn't seem to affect him differently than it did the bed or the chest of drawers: he knew all without knowing anything. The effect of those words became obvious only the day that a column of demonstrators passed by Via Monserrato on the way to a protest rally. The Prince didn't move a finger from the armchair in which he was sitting while Checco with quick steps went to a window which he opened, and over those

56

unusual yells that presumed to shake the most stern and drowsy of streets, as if hoping to awaken it, he waved his arms at the howling crowd.

"It's not you I am against, only that bunch of ruffians who sends you out to scream."

"HEAVENLY WOMAN"

BY THIS NAME was Bice, the doorkeeper to the Prince of Santo Stefano, known in the neighborhood. It was a nickname lacking malicious or teasing intent, yet nobody would have dared to say it in her presence, so that she was totally unaware of it. Not even the street urchins called her that to her face; they were too concerned to stay in her good graces and those of Checco, provider of cakes and cookies whose memory made the tongue click inside the mouth. She was so attracted to and involved in heavenly matters that those of the earth, beyond a certain point, made no impression on her; they had no reason to exist, in fact did not exist. That is why they called her "Heavenly Woman," and also because whenever she had to deal with the practical matters of squalid mankind, she would join her hands over her breast and look skyward with water-colored eyes.

Mail very seldom arrived in the palace, and the little that did was looked upon as importunate and unexpected, bothersome, representative of the many and useless afflictions of life. Letters remained whole days on the top of a small chest next to the door, and once in a while they fell behind it, swallowed by eternity. Or the cat took to playing with them until they were reduced to sawdust. The cat was black and handsome, with golden eyes, renowned for hunting the mice which overflowed the palace from roof to basement. Miss Bice usually kept him sitting in the middle of the table, a place which he himself preferred and where he kept a bearing becoming to a chairman of the board, whether Miss Bice was knitting alone, or with her friends, and even more when in the evenings they recited the rosary all together. Sometimes a telegram arrived, with the looks of a Public Enemy Number One. A telegram? Who can this joker in such a hurry be? Can people be inconsiderate to the point of being in a hurry? The tactless and pompous message would be ushered into a drawer for an unlimited waiting period. That's the way to teach those who are in a hurry. And as the lodgers of the palace were all made of the same dough, it never happened that she would be reproached by anyone. To her went unconditional approval and admiration. Her authority was undisputed.

The same held for the upkeep of the palace, which by now was a large crease, a chasm, a ruin; is the cleaning of a staircase, swept three or four times a year at high holidays, to be taken seriously? Or the fixing of the roof when a gutter breaks? When it rained those living on the last floor had to sleep for several days with open umbrellas, and the whole house would be a mess of pots and pans slowly filling with water. Another piece of molding falling off the facade? When City Hall was about to take action, either she or Checco would go to those offices to counteract the orders through their own higher authority.

By and by, through weddings and funerals, she had found herself in charge alone, in that palace where she had come as a young girl to stay with her brother, the gatekeeper. Once a priest had lived in the palace, an instructor at the Gregoriana University, whose two small rooms tapestried with books she had kept in order for many years; at the point of death, he had left his books to the Gregoriana, and to her the only estate he owned: his clothes, which Miss Bice had been wearing exclusively for a score of years. She even wore the socks, shoes, shirts and shorts of the erstwhile priest. In the rare event that she left the neighborhood to call on some public office she wore his hat, and then she allowed herself to add a teasing flair to its solemnity, by pushing the crown far back and pulling the rim down in front. When she went to a church service she would ask a friendly lodger to stand in for her; if no one could be found she bolted the door and took off as if she had swallowed a torpedo. Everyone knew where she was when her cubicle was closed. She left in her clerical robes, her face covered by a thick veil to show her modesty. In Via Monserrato everybody knew her: "Here is Heavenly Woman," they thought when they perceived her, and, "Good-bye, Missbice," they greeted her aloud. Having descended so low from such height, her answer consisted of a very brief sigh.

Being seventy years old and a spinster, in talking to other women she loudly praised her virginity, never breached even by a forefinger. The neighbors added that she had been left standing because she was frighteningly ugly. The usual lies. There is no woman, ugly that she may be, who can't find a husband if she wants one.

Her room, next to the gateway, was underneath that of the Prince, and of equal size. It had a powerful iron grille on the window facing the street, and against the center wall a chest of drawers used as an altar, on which a small wax light burned eternally between the flowers that solicitous friends brought as an homage, and the forest of candles that were lit only on holidays. Because her duties did not allow her to leave whenever she wanted, she had built up in her room a branch of the parish church, where women lodgers and friends from the neighborhood would gather to discuss and comment on the events of the day: the papal audiences; the services in one parish or another, or in the prodigious cathedrals of Rome— the names of which are enough to spur the imagination; the canonization of a new Saint or Blessed, his earthly vicissitudes; battles, bravery among savages of far-off lands, persecutions that were endured with a faith which feared nothing; pilgrimages to the most famous sanctuaries, of which Miss Bice had a number of souvenirs and mementos, especially candles. When her brother had been alive and she was able to leave for several days, she had walked those roads often enough: the Madonna of Loreto and that of Pompeii, Saint Francis and Saint Clara, Saint Anthony of Padua, the Madonna of Montenero at Leghorn and the one of Saint Luke in Bologna, Saint Rita of Cascia. She even wandered over the mountains of France and Spain to fall on her knees in front of the little white and blue Virgin inside the grotto of Lourdes. From each she had brought back sheaves of candles. There was a trunkful of them; some were extremely beautiful, hand-painted —these she never lit and showed around as relics—the others she burned on great occasions. She lived her last days in great distress. Sometimes, in a moment of confidence, she would reveal it but only to regret it later, for the pain was too great. She preferred to hatch it in silence, alone, which was the only way to feel it less acutely: she hadn't been in the Holy Land. No matter how much she had wished, and tried, she could not materialize her dream. A Christian who has not been in the Holy Land is unfulfilled. Every day he must feel a little bitterness; he never can reach perfect happiness. Never to breathe the air where the Lord's words had resounded, not to set foot on that land where he had walked and carried the cross, where he had let his hands and feet be pierced, where obeying his Father and serving humanity he let himself be crucified for its salvation; and where with a last breath and a word of love for men he rejoined Him. She couldn't even think about these things; it was better not to mention them. They talked, instead, about the activities in the parish church, to which Miss Bice always kept a direct line. Sometimes as she walked into the vestry and found the priest busy with some important matter, she was asked to lead the prayers of the rosary in his stead, both during Mass and at vespers. After the prayers he would come out to give the benediction. It had happened now and again that His Excellency and Checco would be among those who had come to answer her prayers with the utmost devotion, kneeling one next to the other. Napoleon making his entrance in Egypt or Austria did not feel as proud of himself as she did taking the priest's role in church, and having in her congregation the Secret Chamberlain of His Holiness.

After the Ave Maria a tinkling of bells rang through the room on the ground floor and all the floors above. The ringing could be heard even out in the street: *"Ora pro nobis,"* the passersby would answer, joining in. At that time they recited the rosary on every floor. Master and servant alternated on the second floor, on the first Miss Bice and her friends from the parish kept company with each other. Once in a while an ancient priest would appear in the shadow of the door with steps of indiscernible length, and the women without interrupting their recital greeted him swelling with joy, preening themselves around the table on which the handsome black cat presided, a drop of electric light hanging over his head.

Her relations with the Prince, although their hearts beat with the same rhythm, were not nourished by words. When His Excellency saw her, as he walked through the gateway, he went through the motions of lifting his hat off as a mark of respect, adding with his hand a wave of friendship. Checco acted as envoy to the gatekeeper, solving with a few quick words any problem that concerned her. Miss Bice strewed with curtsies the passage of her lord, and when the car with the Vatican plates stopped at the gates to take him to the solemn functions which he was to attend in the Pope's suite, she posted herself half an hour earlier at the door like a guard, until the Prince appeared in his dress uniform. He was even taller in that outfit; he reached unbelievable heights, his legs strikingly thin within the black silk hose that covered them from the small shoes with silver buckles to the balloon of the breeches over the thighs. Above it the chest covered with ruffles, ribbons, and golden galloons, surrounded by a flying little cape, seemed that of a huge butterfly. His face was ghostly as it mirrored the ruffled, starched collar framing it under the feathered hat. Unable to resist, Miss Bice ran to meet him and then followed until he stepped into the car. Her hands joined tightly on her breast, she fluttered in a frenzy, bowing at each step, warming up everything with her movements and gasping breath. Shortwinged, she fluttered inebriated around the king of butterflies. On his master's heels, Checco had become a polliwog. In the left hand the Prince was clutching the sword.

THE
"BARBER
OF
SEVILLE"

THERE WAS a third person in the Prince's household, but he didn't live in the palace and only came there for fifteen minutes every day, at an hour which everyone would have thought to be extremely strange, not to say unlawful; but which in fact was very legitimate and comfortable. Around five-thirty every morning a very short little man could be seen sliding along the walls of Via Monserrato. Only the air and people of exceptional constitution noticed him as he trotted, hugging the walls, wiggling all over in order to keep his minute body warm, and rubbing his hands together. Then, hurried and cold, he reached the great gate under which he disappeared. If someone had been watching him scuttle

64

along from the top of a roof, in the uncertain light of dawn or in complete darkness, he could have thought that it was a dog or a cat running to hide behind that gate after a beating. It was Orazio instead, a barber, and if few had ever seen his passage at that early hour, everyone knew him through myth as "the Barber of Seville," although he lacked any resemblance to or affinity with that character. When the masses yield to imagination, they soar in it. The Prince of Santo Stefano began his day with a quarter hour of relative talkativeness, and even more relative cheer. To be good-humored with his faithful barber was a change, a restful prelude. It was the only luxury he permitted himself, a weakness he hadn't been able to stamp out of his life with the rest. He had often thought of letting his beard grow like that of Moses, but he couldn't forget that his wife, the dead Princess, had disliked bearded men. This had been the only worldly weakness she had ever shown in their married lives, and it related to his own. Orazio worked in almost total darkness, since by now he could have shaved him with eyes closed. And as he felt the blade over his cheeks, the Prince's thoughts fled to the day when he had married the Princess, for whose sake he had strived to look handsome one morning, as now he strove to look handsome in order to receive the Lord after having served Mass.

Checco had offered a hundred times that he would learn how to do it; didn't he shave himself with a free-wheeling razor too? Others had suggested he use a safety razor. Although the Prince did not wish to acknowledge it as such, it was the last luxury he permitted himself; the last and only frivolity, one that in others he would surely have condemned.

As soon as Checco announced: "Orazio, Your Excellency," the Prince, still in his robe, answered warmly: "Come in, Orazio, come in." They exchanged a few words; he commented on the news that Orazio offered him with ceremonious respect,

65

or answered the questions insinuated with shy devotion. Orazio attended Mass only on Sundays, but he rose from bed every morning to shave a Prince who went to serve one. He received a ridiculous compensation for his pains: the Prince had never been able to catch up with the cost of life and tarried forever among the prices of antiquity. Checco, Bice and Orazio hardly got any pay; the honor of serving him was their compensation, the greatness that rubbed off on them. If Orazio did not feel a need to go to Mass every morning, it was because after having made the sacrifice of awakening with the birds he felt sanctified and that was enough to repay him; he almost felt that it was he who owed something.

Scuttling out of the great gate and disappearing along the walls Orazio returned home to get back in bed. A few minutes afterwards the hatch in the gate opened again, to let His Excellency and Checco pass on their way to Mass.

THE
SUNLIT
CITY

IN THE COUNTRYSIDE it is the
birds that herald the coming of the sun.

They start singing as soon as the deep blue of the night
melts into grayness and the stars begin to fade. It is a twitter
that rises, at first almost unnoticed through sleep, with a few
short and shy chirps which in the still, even quiet announce a
vital movement and gain altitude; then a longer and stronger
chirping spreads over the fields as stars spread over the sky
in the evening. From one branch to the next, from one tree
to the other, from hill to hill . . . into an ever-stronger and
more insistent, full-throated song. It seems that the tiny bodies
contain only a melody until the sun soothes them by placing

a golden halo over those little heads that have proclaimed at his rising the happiness of life. One wonders whether the most brilliant conductor isn't somewhere leading that symphony. No: the conductor has been there once for all time, and the performance has been perfect ever since.

In Rome the sun is ushered in by bells, their voices dissimilar in tone, pitch and volume. From the bells of the little church next to where you live the words fall fast: "Wake up, get up, hurry up, off the bed, haven't you slept enough, what are you still doing there"—to the big bell of St. Peter's, whose voice is warm and impressive, expanding in wider and wider circles in a radius that defies computation, and blends with the upper regions of space. The Roman can recognize the voices of bells as that of people; he listens to them dozing or falling into that fragile but so pleasant last light sleep, which completes the long restoring one. Mind and body are enveloped in down; from there he listens to the sound of bells that cradles him, he falls into listening without having to make efforts to think, it's too early to think. He never rises five minutes too early, and he awakens only a bit, just enough to hear the bells. It never crosses his mind to hurry up, but he likes that sound and begins to move under the blankets as the birds do among the leaves of trees, enjoying the last part of conscious rest before starting his daily labors; he rises surrounded by sweetness and splendor.

In the thick of the city, over still-empty streets, where only the passage of the first bus seemingly sledding on the pavement breaks the silence, men take over the task of the birds. Those few who rush on foot or on bicycle towards early jobs go whistling by. In the emptiness that seems their own they release the health of their lungs in a whistle that skims over roofs, breaks through walls into shuttered rooms. They know how to whistle, like the nightingales, jay birds, finches. "Nobody will see me, but they are all going to hear me," thinks the lone walker, putting more zest in his whistling, and often in the fresh air of the first dawn his whistle blends with the sound of bells.

"I die despairing..."

but hastens to add:

"Yet I have never loved life more."

The first being a poetic lie; the second, truth.

"Oy Mari, oy Mari..."

Once outside he doesn't envy those still warmly sleeping, although he doesn't mind waking them up if he can; but above all he likes to be heard, to let it be known that he is happy, that he is there.

"Murmured the Piave..."

Lustier than ever, the whistling means that after having won over laziness, man will walk toward another happiness, that of greeting in the pure air the hatching day.

There are the best-known operatic arias, pop songs, old favorites and latest hits, anthems. As long as silence allows it, the eager citizen of Rome will fill it with the warmth of his breast.

Not even this second reveille will hasten by one minute those who are still under blankets; on the contrary, hearing others whistle in the street they snuggle up even closer. But they enjoy hearing the voices as pleasant as those of the birds; they like to listen in half-sleep as they listened earlier to the bells.

The sunlit city is not an early riser. Those who pass by whistling a little before or after dawn don't do it voluntarily: they are compelled by necessity. Why hurry when there will be so many hours in which to relish the sun?

From the tolling of bells and the whistling through the air cleared by the night, to the full movement of day some more hours have to pass, while the air becomes heavier and heavier. But the sun is busy changing into gold the dust raised by men with the weight of their labors; those whom you see walking on the streets do not seem to have any business or to be seeking any: they seem to be just taking a walk, to be watching how other people walk, speak, how they are dressed. They look at the shopwindows, meet friends and acquaintances, they stop for a chat and linger for long discussions on the sidewalks and in the crowded streets, as if they were in a living room, quietly unconcerned about obstructing the traffic which becomes ever more complex and worrisome. In the poorer districts young men congregate on corners and at the doors of coffee-houses —which they attend with the same perseverance the English devote to their clubs—to discuss movies and sport, sport especially. They talk about the soccer teams of Rome and Lazio, and about girls: they know all the girls in the neighborhood, they don't miss any details, they are aware of every bit of news that concerns them; the boys of Rome know how to enjoy women, they enjoy all of them in thought and with their eyes. And the girls who pass by those groups pretending indifference and excessive haste know that they are leaving behind a wake of interest and awe; they try to make themselves more pretty to tease them. Smiles bloom like daisies on a field in springtime, growing from an irrepressible desire to forget what constitutes the heavy loads of life. Underneath everything shines a warmly responsive happiness, rooted in well-kneaded flesh of handsome color. Flesh untroubled by twitching nerves or by the tyranny of the mind, looking for its likes, attracting them; a vital flesh, ready to be touched and whose touch doesn't produce revulsion, irritation, or worry; it has a healthy strength, serene and natural.

At certain hours in the buses, at the so-called rush hours, one could say that human flesh achieves a single identity. Especially in summer with light clothes, those of the women extremely light: it is obvious that the tireless defenders of morals all travel by car. There is a subtle art of positioning oneself.

Jostling is universal. It would, in fact, seem the civic institution dearest to the heart of Romans; in order to buy a stamp you have to shove and be shoved. The foreigner who happens to be caught in it, unable to move, feeling people walk over his feet, will puff, strain, and rave under the sincerely compassionate stare of the Roman, who thinks with a smile more luminous than the sun: "Poor wretch, you look like a soul in Hell, can't you see that I am in Heaven?"

Thus the hours go by in the sunlit city, as household tasks unfold in the homes awash with light and on the terraces. There is no house without a number of terraces on its roofs. Every lodger has one and sometimes two or three: on them they grow plants as in gardens; one can find full-grown trees, vineyards, and all sorts of fruits as in the times of Semiramis; ivy and oleanders hang from them, letting their blinding beauty overflow the light. They compel upward one's admiring gaze. An Oriental life goes on in the houses of Rome, and on the terraces where people study, work, cook meals, eat, dance, entertain, wash linen, sing and make love. The ideal quarters in this town are two rooms on a terrace blooming with flowers.

And there are two periods each year when the air and light produce a painful passion in your soul: the yearning of Spring which meets your desire anticipating it by at least a month, and the months of Fall when Summer lingers and seems, like youth, to want to live forever—it falls so often yet each time gathers new strength, you think it extinguished and yet it isn't, until Winter's threshold.

If the city of the sun is not an early riser, neither is it a night owl. It would be a ghastly mistake to come here expecting to lead a night life: all the beauty of its late mornings, the fascinating last hours of afternoon—would be lost, and nothing found in its stead. In Rome people sleep at night, the few night clubs exist in utter disrepute and isolation, like leprosaries; they seem to be ashamed of themselves as if branded by infamy. They have nothing interesting or attractive, and their very slight pleasures are for people who come from outside. Romans are not even aware that there are places where one lives at night. Matinees of any kind are overcrowded; nightly shows, unless they are exceptional, have few customers; and when they let out people seem to suffer from the pains of darkness. At nine o'clock in the evening life ends for the citizens of the sunlit city, everybody returns home, eats supper and goes to bed, just like hens.

THE
MOON

SOMEONE MIGHT ask: "So nobody enjoys the moon in Rome?"

The moon gives pleasure to few people.

One would say that Romans remain indifferent to the romantic godhead of night, whom they prefer to leave to its pastures undisturbed by their curiosity. If they happen to meet it they don't pause to show feeling or love, nor do they express aversion or hate: among the many things one can see there is the moon, and to it they say with a shiver that makes their steps hasten instinctively: "It's time to go to bed." Man of warmth, the Roman doesn't like cold things, in-between colors—he likes to see shapes with hard edges and full light, he never

73

thinks there can be too much light, dislikes shadows and shade, looks for darkness only when demographic needs come to a boil.

The privilege of enjoying the moon in all of its beauty is reserved to the foreigner, and connoisseurs of this kind should be obliged to the Romans.

Very few people are on the streets. The widest ones appear to be empty; Romans who are never in a hurry and take such pleasure in seeing and being seen become harried at night and can only think of hiding: the peacock has become a squirrel who doesn't care what's around him.

The squares that teem during the day, so crowded that they seem to overflow, are at night opened in unusual shapes; empty, they leave you speechless by their silence. This book could not describe their number and variety: there are one hundred thirty-five of them. Under the moon their dimensions change. Some large ones coil up and become small, some that appeared to be only large become immense, the immense lose their bounds, the eye can't reach their sides.

Under the shining pallor mankind sleeps, every semblance of movement vanishes; these shapes only are awake to confide their secret to the lone lover. The observer has the feeling that this show was made especially for him.

Human voices do not sound well in Rome at night, worse if they are shrill, thoughtless or carefree: they create intolerable harshness and dissonance, trivial curses; they harmonize if they are low, no more than whispers, far between and quiet: the watchful stillness is for thinking only.

Arches and columns, stairways, domes and obelisks, the statues—all so friendly and familiar until the last red shades of twilight disappear, when they are approached with full confidence, their stones merging with the human body whose flesh leans against them, finds rest and sleep on them—after the fall of darkness take on forms and colors that make you feel inferior, force you to stand up and go away. A layer of cold mistrust arises between them and man, forcing the passerby into silence and concentration.

Moonlit night in Rome is not romantic. It suggests nothing vague or sentimental; emotion does not take over. It is thought that takes the helm and steers you, that crowds and impels you on the Capitol or Quirinal Squares, does not permit you to relent, not even when you are in the square with three fountains built like a ship where in daytime hundreds of children shout the pure drunkenness of life as if they were at home. Leaning over into dark silence you feel so shy of the overwhelming void that it is a task to cross it and to find its end. And in St. Peter's Square, where the eyes cannot escape the precise, well-defined limits which are visible in any light, the glance is riveted in order to support the soaring flight of thought. The roaring fountains offer the refreshment of a sweet restful slumber. Not even among the ruins, where one would most expect it, is the moon romantic: the light unveils them only to bring forth a crowd of piercing thoughts; not even on the Appian Way, that sooner or later will make you wonder in which direction it is taking you. Never a moment of romanticism—a misplaced sense of limits oscillating somewhere between Heaven and earth—the mind does not descend below ground to get lost in its entrails, nor does it ascend to Heaven to search for a higher, deeper, greater task.

THE
DUKE
OF
ROVI

CHECCO HAD BEEN a little over twenty and in the Prince's service a short while when Gherardo, Duke of Rovi, third child and only male offspring of Prince Filippo of Santo Stefano, was born. He took part in the rejoicing at the heir's birth, rejoicing on the part of the parents and the little sisters Elisabetta and Maria Adelaide, for whom Dado—the nickname they used from the very first day—became the center of interest and care, devout and protective affection, and childish curiosity. He became heir to the family honor which, thanks to a rigid sense of integrity, had remained unblemished for seven centuries. This was his first and only heritage, since the patrimony of the house, thinned through the ages, was on the point of exhaustion, not due to recklessness or indolence, but because of fateful external events and, above all, because of the stern principle of inflexibility towards any kind of compromise with life and society. The future Prince was to become of age at the time that his father would have spent on him and on his sisters the last savings.

The Duke of Rovi was thirty-eight years old, and for fifteen of them he had been living abroad.

At first he had pressured his father to obtain money from him, and had had a vague view of settling down somewhere as soon as he would receive his degree in law; as long as he was able his father complied, refraining from asking assurances that would have been humiliating to both of them. When the young Duke realized the well had dried up and further requests would have been useless, he limited himself to sending his father sporadic news, taking care that they should be always good, excellent, the best, without mentioning even vaguely his way of life and the boundless designs that he once had. No one knew where he found the means to achieve the lush life he led, always moving from one country to the next. At first his father wrote long letters encouraging him to return to a solid and dignified position that would have been easy for him to find through his many friendships and contacts; he even hinted at the possibility of marriage to a childhood friend with a renowned name and a father who, although also impoverished, was still able to give his daughter a modest dowry.

Having explored the horizon, his poor nobility and the useless doctorate, the proposed wedding entailing much honor but little cash—and moreover to a woman he didn't care for as a wife—the young Duke peremptorily left his father's home, making it clear that he preferred to roam the world searching for that which comes to those who will not tire of roaming, rather than live in monotony a second-rate life in the shadow of a faded and dusty crown.

When he stopped for a few days in Rome, he made a point of calling on his father, as it's done between friends. During such visits father and son would face each other doing everything they could to say nothing while they talked, without a trace of trust, or a hint that could reveal a glimmer of reality, or a question that could embarrass the other. Sophistication imbued with irony on the part of the young gentleman; on that of the old, an unvoiced and irrepressible fear of hearing things that would wound him deeply, he who in every action of his life was so sure of himself, always so confident.

Since the beginning of the war, eight years earlier, the Prince hadn't seen his son.

Through short and infrequent letters or news given by his daughters, he knew that Dado was well—they still called him that, as when they used to hide toys or sweets from him to see him cry, and then laugh when the objects reappeared. The news always came from a different part of Europe, Africa, or Asia Minor. So when Checco, standing on the threshold, quavered: "The young master," he was trembling with joy: he found again the carefree young voice of so long ago, when Gherardo used to climb on his knees, or order him to be taken for a walk—not being allowed to go alone he wanted to go only with Checco, because with him he could do whatever he wanted—and Checco like a compliant older child would let himself be taken around by that eager child greedy for learning, happy in seeing the other happy. But the Prince, upon hearing the graceful and unexpected words that made his servant's lips tremble for joy, felt an icy current run through his body, from the roots of his hair to the soles of his shoes. The man always so assured, who never hesitated to express his feelings, principles or ideas, who in all cases made his position clear, had always felt this cold chasm that nothing had succeeded in bridging between himself and his son. He had in fact become shy with him, cautious, unsure of what to say —a man who had had words ready even when addressed by the Pope. So he stood up as if wanting to boast of the height of his body, and assumed the attitude of a monument.

"*Ciao*, Daddy," greeted the son with cheerful impetuousness, similar to the way in which he used to come in to greet his father after school, but too informally for someone who had been away for eight years. Although close to middle age, the Duke had kept the bearing of youth at its best. His strong, handsome, truly Roman brown face was three times sweetened: by the elegant gentleness of his movements, the tastefulness of his clothes and, more than anything else, by a tender sensuality of character. He looked ten years younger than his age, and warmth radiated from his eyes, hinting at a permanent invitation. Instead of thawing the Prince, as it did everyone else, such handsome geniality seemed to be made to purpose to cool him further down to a polar temperature. The Prince was changed to salt. The more he felt chill in his bones and the snail's instinct of hiding in his shell at the time of misgiving, the stronger an effort he made to erect his body as much as he could, as if stature were the last resource against his son.

"I haven't been able to write but rarely and a few lines during this long and unfortunate period, both because of the factual difficulties that you know as well as I do, and also because I kept traveling from one country to the next, on the spur of the moment and without any plans . . . ." Then he turned around, slightly overcome by the sternness of the environment, and glanced at his father's cot pushed against the wall. "But have you been forced into this room? Have you left the rest of the house, sold the furniture?"

"What could I have done with house and furniture once I was left alone? I left everything to those who had more need of it than I did. I kept the hall and this room for myself, and Checco's little room behind mine, that's all I need."

"I see, I see, of course," Duke Gherardo drew out the words, as if ready to abandon himself to the alluring drowsiness that radiated from the place and the things in it, a too well known place, which at the same time, after so many years, appeared so strange, so incredible and typical, too typical: "I see . . . the throne . . . and a monk's bed."

"Exactly." After an instant of silence Prince and Duke sat down facing each other. "The throne and a monk's bed."

"A slightly funny combination, but it doesn't matter. Don't you think, dear Daddy, that these things don't go well together?"

"Why? For Christians of our rank, they are in perfect harmony."

"Yes, indeed. . . . When I was in Jerusalem I remembered you, I thought a lot about you, about the tales of your travels in the Holy Land that you used to tell us when we were children, the pilgrimages of your youth. But nowadays, unfortunately, the whole world has only one aim, except for a few souvenirs of the past which are being more and more isolated, one wonders whether because of arrogance or shame at the sadness of their decrepit old age. The things that are being done in Jerusalem are not much different from those being done in Rome, New York, Berlin, Paris, everywhere. A hundred years more and all cities will resemble each other with enervating sameness, with gray, uniform flatness."

The Duke mouthed words upon words, as if he wanted to warm up the room with his breath; the Prince in front of him sat in the attitude of one who is willing to listen uncommitted to the conversation.

"But, Daddy, I haven't come to talk of cities, houses, or

architecture, whether ancient or modern, but to give you important news. Of course, being the right and respectful thing, you are the first to hear about it: I am going to get married." The sureness with which the Duke of Rovi uttered his last words increased the father's watchfulness so that he withheld his breath; the privilege bestowed on him did not bring any sign of assent to his features, nor any other intelligible expression. "I know very well what you are thinking, I should have taken this step long ago, yes, I should have been married who knows since when. I am aware of that, yet I couldn't say exactly why it has been like this. Up to now I haven't felt any need for it, to be frank the idea had never before entered my head, as if such a widespread and deserving institution didn't even exist, or perhaps I had never met the person who would have been able to remind me of it. Today on the other hand the idea has entered my head, it has taken over in there, and achieved a place of prominence: I found the person, that's why I am getting married. I am marrying a Syrian dancer, but she has spent most of her life in Europe, she has danced in all the European theaters, so that she is actually European. Her name is Magda. A very beautiful woman, Daddy, very beautiful and intelligent, of that instinctive intelligence—perhaps physical is a better word—women sometimes have, and through which they can get whatever they want. A fascinating creature, a champion of the species. The qualities of the Jewish race are distilled in her, with all the contributions of our Western culture in their most exquisite and delicate shadings. I first saw her when she was dancing in a Cairo theater three years ago: I was stupefied, enchanted, her image stayed engraved in my memory so that I could think only of her, I saw her wherever I turned my eyes, time couldn't erase it, I dreamed about her every night. And when by chance I met her again I became completely enthralled as I had never been to that day.

81

In Damascus we met again; there Magda owns a splendid villa left to her, with an infinity of other things, by a fabulously rich old Jewish friend who discovered her poor and very young, still a child, in a Hamburg vaudeville. Although she is rich now, Magda hasn't given up her art, nor will she do so: she loves it with a passion—after all she drew from it success and fortune. She also does religious dances; you should see her, Daddy, dressed as St. Theresa or the Magdalene. You would really like her, she looks like one of the angels in the churches of Rome, by Bernini or someone from his Baroque school: she's a marvel, a genius; what an artist. She would make you cry, Daddy. And right after that she does a Spanish dance with which she fills the stage like a storm that gives you vertigo, a heat that spreads fire; or a Negro dance she does in the nude, and takes your breath away just as she does with the religious dance. Now we live in Paris where Magda owns a flat left her also by the old Jewish friend; right now she is preparing a contract for an American tour. The hour has come that Magda wants to get married; well, she can't understand this herself, her condition is the same as mine, identical to it: she too has thought of it for the first time, yes, she wants a husband. Her ambition couldn't be more natural; after all, it is that of all women, and Magda, though rich and no matter how adventurous her life has been, is still a girl. We are exactly of the same age, both born in 1910—this I confide to your discretion as a secret because Magda, like all women, never says the truth and claims ten years less. She wants a husband: that's right. She is tired of being thought of as a spinster, as all of them are. Talent and fortune notwithstanding, she will give up gladly part of her independence to have a husband. And probably her secret unconfessed ambition is to raise herself through marriage to a title—she never said so, but she makes it clear that she is very glad to become a princess, a Roman princess.

And she plays delightfully with this thought, like a cat playing with yarn. A title that would crown her legendary person and brilliant career. She has everything to carry it in a way that few who were born with it could match. She wants a prominent place in society after having had it on the stage; the whim of a smart and beautiful woman who has succeeded in everything. In whatever situation she finds herself, Magda knows how to use all her talents to triumph over life. Daddy, I am possessed and seduced by the very thought, I am committed to make it true. I cannot describe to you how comforted I am to be able to tell all this to you first, before anyone else. You understand that our wedding will be celebrated in Rome. It's here we plan to keep our permanent address, although for the greater part of the year we will be traveling. We will also keep the flat in Paris and the villa in Damascus—Magda is very attached to it, she says that she could never leave it no matter what. It's very natural, it's just too beautiful. You should see the swan pond, what a dream, and the green kiosk where one can eat in every season of the year—it's heaven. And there Magda, barefoot, does the classical dances that make one dream of the splendor of Greece, make one believe he is breathing the scents of the Orient."

While the Duke of Rovi talked with affected inspiration and even less genuine ease, the Prince's eyes had dilated until they filled his whole face, and after breaking the banks of his face, filled the whole body and the room. Facing his son, he was no more than two unmeasurably large eyes. And when he said a few words, taking advantage of an interruption, these were striking for the utter quiet with which they were pronounced. That which could have been a turbulent flow overturning everything in its path appeared as a placid little blue lake under a clear pink sky. A place where on a summer noon you can't feel a breath of air.

"Even if you married that woman ten times, she would not be your wife. Save yourself the effort and tell her right away that even married ten times she will never become the Duchess of Rovi, or still less likely, the Princess of Santo Stefano. It's an adventure, only an adventure for the worldly people to slide over with malicious greed; men, like flies, are easily attracted by dirt; but honest men pass on."

"I won't be so silly as to tell Magda anything that might throw off our plans."

"Plans like these end always by being thrown off, they exist in the air, having lacked from the moment of their inception a legitimate basis."

"And why shouldn't I marry this woman?"

"It's useless for me to say since you know it as well as I do, precisely as I do."

The Duke of Rovi raised a clouded face.

"Who can prevent me?"

"No one can prevent you and no one will; mistakes are being made every day, even bigger than yours."

"Is it perhaps because Magda is a dancer? Dance, like all other arts, is very noble; and she is an artist."

"I have never doubted the nobility of the arts, dance included; but your nobility is something else again."

"Perhaps because she is Jewish?"

It seemed that the Prince felt an answer useless, so the Duke went on:

"I was told that years ago, during the German occupation, you opened your house to the Jews, turning it into a camp of Israel."

"Certainly. And I would do it again if it were necessary, without an instant of hesitation. As a Christian I offer my power and strength to right an injustice, no matter who are involved. At the time when blind fury had seized the soul of some people till they had fallen to the level of beasts that live in the forest, my conscience told me to help them, save them without one thought for my safety or my very life. This house was made into a Jewish camp, exactly. They slept with their children on those steps which popes used to climb. I am ready to open my house again every time injustice is done to them."

"And do you think that those Jews love you after you saved their lives?"

"That doesn't concern me, it concerns them. I did my duty, that's enough for me."

"They hate you even more. And they are right because while their hate is genuine, your charity isn't."

The Prince tightened his lips as if determined not to grant another answer.

"That's it, I see. A Christian can be so good as to offer asylum to the Jews in the hour of danger, to prepare for them bedding at night and soup in the morning, perhaps even to serve it with the utmost humbleness; but he will never shake their hand on an equal plane. That's why I should not marry a Jewish woman."

"I already told you that I don't have to explain why you shouldn't marry a Jewish woman. Nor do I have to remind you that there have been neither dancers nor Jews among the women of your family."

"Exactly. You only confirm what I said just now. But perhaps this is the mistake, dear Daddy, yes, it is for sure: our family has never had dancers or Jews till now, or things of that kind that could have rescued it. But all those things that as good Christians you have banished, ostracized with such severity, are preparing their revenge and will fall on your head all at once: dancers, Jewesses ... and worse things probably. Time acts alone by itself, unswaying and relentless executioner of our way of life. When not supported by money,

85

a coat of arms becomes a butt for jokes fit for the storage-room of a pawnshop."

"A coat of arms can be supported only by complete honesty, without any misunderstandings, double meanings, compromises; otherwise it becomes with reason an object for scorn and ridicule. If the man who should be of example cheats, what should those who are called to follow him do? You too have fallen for the fallacy of our times: to have put foremost scraps of paper."

Gherardo laughed patronizingly.

"Dear Daddy, one cannot do a thing without those scraps: nobody, unless he is resigned to disappear in the shadows and to let the mold grow on his body. Even the Church, like everyone else, needs a goodly amount of those scraps. Yes! But the likes of you won't admit it. You have mastered the art of drawing wine from the kegs, and when something falls into your ravenous jaws it completely disappears. The account is always in balance and the scraps of paper leave no trace."

In order not to let transpire the unease to which he felt prey, the Prince increased in serenity.

"As you know well, the Church lives in the world. It needs material means for its subsistence and for the infinite and ever-growing number of institutions it runs: the Church has to practice charity."

"Exactly, exactly . . . ." The Duke answered musingly as if he were gathering words scattered in his brain, like dry leaves swept by the wind on days heralding winter. "Exactly . . . after faith and therefore hope have been lost—you have seen them vanish into thin air one after the other—you have replaced them with the entirely wordly virtue of charity. You are on the last step."

"We haven't replaced anything. The theological virtues form an inseparable whole."

"Yes, but man is getting tired of receiving alms. He requires his share to be given as a right, demands what is due to him without having to thank anyone, without having to kiss any man's hands or slippers. Unfortunately there are still people in this world, too many of them, alas, who ask nothing better than to grovel, to kneel, to humiliate themselves before another person, to kiss hands and feet; if one were to introduce the notion of having his ass kissed he would obtain an unmatched success, people would come from the North Pole, they would throng for the kissing; but their number is luckily diminishing every day."

"Charity is the substance of Christian life, in any time and every place, under whatever circumstances it has to be practiced."

"Right, but not this way. Your charity is tainted because you never give away a mouthful unless it's followed by a homily, your free soup is paid for exorbitantly and it's always bitter. I prefer the one I eat at the inn; thief that the owner might be, it's cheaper than yours. No innkeeper has ever asked a soul for a soup. But that's not what I meant to talk about. Let's get back to what we were saying before: it would have been better, I said, if there had been a dancer or someone of that sort before now to keep your shack from falling as low as it is now. At this point, if all the saints at your disposal haven't succeeded, it won't be easy for a dancer to perform the miracle."

The Prince straightened proudly, and without losing composure raised a forefinger above his head:

"My shack is flawless, no one has been nor will be able to besmear it."

"Your blindness, that of all of you who belong to a doctrine doggedly pursued, is either pure cynicism practiced in utter bad faith, refusing to acknowledge reality, factual evidence, or is due to weakness of mind, in which case a man like you should be locked in an asylum as a danger to society. Let's draw a balance of your shack and let's see how far it's faultless and spotless. Maria Adelaide made a nun of herself, no question about it, she was like you, she said 'no' to life, she hated life and she goes on hating it in the grace of the Lord, forgetting that it was the Lord who gave her life."

"She said 'no' to the life of the senses in order to devote herself to that of the spirit: Maria Adelaide is a chosen soul."

"She might be as chosen as you like, Daddy, so far no argument; however, you will admit that she has shirked an unquestionable commandment that mother nature has given her very clearly. She has in her body a certain organ whose function is to reproduce the species; she is entitled not to use it, to take it out of the running—she can salt away part of herself or her whole body, she is free to do it—but if all the women were to do like she did you understand that your show would be up."

"Naturally only a few exceptional beings of a privileged nature can do it, it's a unique vocation, a divine call. They represent a superior world, the highest part of mankind."

"No, no, let's not fly too high up, nothing as special as you think. One would say you haven't looked around even in the world in which you live, you haven't taken the trouble. The majority of women in religious orders have chosen the nunnery rather than working as maids or in a factory, or working the soil, or facing the hardships of a poor family life."

"And they become mothers to everyone, since all are in need of them."

"It is slightly different to be mothers to everyone whenever you please and without personal involvement, instead of being mother to half a dozen children. Having to worry about their upkeep, their education, and their future."

"They practice motherhood in a hundred practical ways,

besides that higher form of motherhood which is that of the soul."

"Yes, I know, I know, but can't you see, dear Daddy, I couldn't care less for this rarefied life of the soul, and so that you may understand me better, I will say it as they say in Rome: I piss on it. I am interested in the life men live every-day on this earth. I am more modest; the higher life of the spirit I leave to you. That belongs to the world of daydreams, of fantasy; and I prefer to live in reality. As you see I can get along with less."

"You have fallen into a materialism that is frightening, painful, horrifying, that sets tyrannical limits to your life."

"Materialism does set tyrannical limits, I agree, but not as many as you people do with your spirituality, and they are completely arbitrary; that's why we are materialists. On one side bare spirit, on the other bare matter: these two currents are destined to fight relentlessly, the reason why Christianity can be summarized by twenty centuries of struggle."

"Not physical struggle: Christians cannot and do not kill."

"Well, you are perfectly right, you haven't killed many with your own hands, but only because you have always found someone to do the killing for you. It's obvious that you are the first ones not to believe in a future life, otherwise you would know that the debt is yours and that you will have to settle it. But let's return to the point: you want to know why Maria Adelaide refused life? Because, just like you, she hates life: deep down your unavowed pleasure is not to let others enjoy it either, to take it away from others with very refined cunning, with devilish malice; to scare them, discourage them with life, to use every means to make it look hateful, ugly, evil, painful, unworthy to be lived. And you keep trying to trip up those who decide to live anyway, you hate those who love and understand it, who enjoy it despite all; you don't spare any effort to diminish, to soil it, saying ill of what's beautiful and pleasant, limiting its possibilities, squashing or deflating its joys, perverting its values, and all this in such wailing tones that it ends by stifling thought, your relentless enemy. Beggary is your ally, it permits you to give charity; intelligence is your enemy. To repeat millions upon millions of times the same word, until the mind befogs, paralyzed, reduced to barrenness; until the other, tired and confused, unable to think, agrees with you. 'I am unable, forbidden to understand and enjoy life because of an inborn incapacity, a racial misfortune; therefore others must not enjoy it either.' It's your vengeance. Have everybody hate and despise it, or if you can't accomplish that, then have them at least hate it outwardly, in words, pretending to shun it but enjoying it on the sly, in concealment, so that on their deathbeds they should feel they had been vulgar thieves, and life a heinous theft of which they must repent; that at least with their last breath all should utter their 'no.' Frightened in the face of the unknown by your mournful presence, everyone will certainly say it: what a victory! You know what such a deed as yours is called in the law books? Blackmail. That is why you like to live in hospitals, in jails, wherever people cry and suffer, among the cancer of mankind, where life has become unbearable. And it isn't love that moves you: love is only a passport to you. It's pleasure for what makes life sad and negative. You are perfect sadists. Aren't you afraid that the Lord will ask you to account for the miserable use you have made of His gift, for having so utterly misunderstood? You have damaged the human race more with your false virtue than all the passions, crimes and sins put together. You have falsified everything, so that nobody believes any more, there is nothing in which one believes, as soon as one opens his mouth to talk your first thought is to know what's behind it, what's underneath, everyone fears to be deceived, cheated, and defends himself by deceiving and cheating in his turn. Double-talk is now learned by infants at the breast; there is an endless number of chances to practice it, with an art worthy of better cause. The world that you created is a mess of factions engaged in damaging each other without heeding personal or collective interest; as long as yours exists things will always be the same, because of all the factions yours is the blackest, the others are made in your image."

The Prince had passed the point up to which his son's words would have had influence over his soul, and he now listened with Olympian peace, almost on the point of laughing—unusual event indeed in the chronicles of Via Monserrato.

"I haven't said 'no' to life, as shown by the fact I was married and had four children."

"Yes, you were one of those who made love through a hole in the nightgown."

"There weren't any holes in my nightgown nor in those of your mother. I have given you an education similar to that of everybody else in good society. You went to school and learned what you pleased to learn—for this purpose I spent the last resources of our family. I haven't said 'no' to life, and I haven't done anything to take it away from my children."

"Only because you were not able to. Your innermost desire had been to create this nucleus and drag it down with you into the world of mummies, in an ever-tightening circle, to find renunciation in these shady rooms that are a delight to you, but make a normal person shudder. You haven't taken life away from us because we didn't let you, we weren't made for darkness but to live in sunlight. One after the other we escaped, and you couldn't reach us. You did succeed with your favorite daughter, but you failed with the rest. I remember the day Maria Adelaide took the veil: I had never seen your face shine so much before, it was resplendent, you couldn't contain your happiness—while I felt a knot tightening in my throat and had to make efforts not to cry."

"It was certainly a more beautiful day than the one you make me live through today."

"It's you who wanted this day, it's your work and it had to happen, it's your masterpiece. You can't bring up someone to be a prince and then expect him to become a flunky who has to work under a fussy boss, or to be paid by a newly rich bourgeois who enjoys your daily subservience to the hilt. But let us go on exploring the horizon. Betty and Bill, as you know, or as you see, have lived for twenty years very expensively; when they call on you in your lair they drive the latest custom-made luxury job, they dress according to the rules, they live in the best hotels—who gives them the money for it? Have you never asked yourself? Betty didn't have a cent, your dowry may have been enough for a month, Billy was worse off than ever. When he was a young man in Naples he was caught red-handed cheating in his club. In deference to his name and because of the intervention of some influential people the thing was hushed up. So he decided to move to Rome where no family considered him an eligible bachelor except ours; here it was easy, there was nothing to lose. They live among more or less rotten, equivocal people, or the newly rich who use their name to force open closed doors, who pay their hotel bills, their tailors, and for the custom-made cars. They gamble and lend themselves to any deals: the more at stake, the more they like it. They aren't caught red-handed any more because everybody knows that their cooperation has to be paid somehow. I don't think such behavior is in line with your plans or your taste. And here is the heir to all your titles, a list that never ends, heir to your name and your nobility: living abroad for fifteen years, kept by women."

"And you would accuse me of such baseness? I have never taken money from women, not even from your mother, who had been as poor as I was."

"You haven't been kept by women, but you have produced one who is, and quite well too. You know: a handsome boy, cheerful, pleasant and witty, of undisputable nobility. It was very easy, it went by itself. But you know what a man like myself is called? A gigolo—of a certain class of course, but different only in appearance from the ones you see waiting on the corners of ill-famed streets. Now that I start to fade—shortly I will be thirty-eight, and for certain purposes the years begin to be a little too many—I have only one expedient left: to get married. That's the purpose of my visit, to announce my marriage. Oh yes, I almost forgot your last daughter: Norina. She has escaped into a middle-class marriage. You know as well as I do what the Sequis are. They made unknown millions in a few decades through the two wars. They are one of the richest families in Rome, some even say the richest. The mother hails from swineherds and milk-farmers of the Po Valley, and doesn't try to hide it; on the contrary, she is loudly complacent about it. Well, she is a woman who knows her business, you only have to look at her to imagine her satisfaction in visiting her father's yards to see a thousand pigs slaughtered. The father comes from an old family of Roman builders, 'miscellaneous constructions,' that can mean houses or toothbrushes. With scruples one cannot make millions, dear Father, prayers won't help either: scruples and prayers are the quickest road to death by starvation. You know how much they criticize and question the Sequi fortune. For twenty years they have been hankering after a title of nobility but they won't give it to them yet, no matter what they do they don't want to give in; after all, a title would be a little too much for profiteers with both hands dirtied by very legal and respectable frauds. But with time they will have that too, I'm sure, probably through practicing charity; they will have to stretch their necks, but eventually they will have their title. To begin with they bought themselves a princess, your youngest daughter, whom they show off among the precious objects of their house as if she were a talisman, a point on which to get leverage, yet at the same time they despise her and treat her rudely. They know she won't go away. Where could she go, without a penny? And with a house like yours to return to. But your life is still unblemished. You have the Pope's throne, what else could you need?" He looked around the lower part of the room: "Don't you have a cat? It's a real shame. He could have beautiful dreams on it."

The Duke of Rovi stood up, and the Prince joined him without showing anger or surprise, or the faintest embarrassment.

"Now that we have reviewed ourselves I won't disturb you any longer. Forgive me, Daddy, but this visit before my marriage was a necessity. Probably it will be the last: some things last for a lifetime and it's useless to repeat them. Be in good health and I will try to do the same; good-bye."

Without a gesture of leavetaking, the Duke of Rovi turned about and left.

Crossing the throne hall he looked at the great canopy and started to laugh in a high register, a strident laugh resembling the cry of crows. To Checco, who came to meet him with unusual haste, he said:

"I am the heir to the throne."

"Are you joking? You are the heir to everything."

"No, no, that's too much, Checco, the throne is enough, what else would I need?"

And he went on with his high-pitched laugh.

From his little room Checco had heard everything; not a

shadow of fear or resentment showed on his face, but a smile more lively than ever. He loved the young master with a love that ignored doubt. He had loved him from the day he was born. He had been so happy to give in to the spirited and imperious boy that no matter what he could do to himself or to the adored Prince, he would not resent or reproach it; he would have done anything to save him, to give him shelter— it was the only person with whom he felt weak. The unshakable certitude he had with everyone else gave way when he faced the young master; if he had killed him, with a six-inch blade deep in his chest, Checco would have asked, with his last shining smile: "Master, why did you do it?" He followed behind him to the door and called to his back: "See you soon, Master." The other answered without turning, his voice normal once again:

"Good-bye, Checco, take care."

He followed him with his eyes to the bottom of the staircase and beyond, when he was already out of sight; then he slowly closed the door, as if to close it were painful to him. With his duck-steps he ambled back through the throne hall to the room of the Prince, who was facing the window pane with closed eyes. When his eyes were open, they were ovens that burned his body like timber; when they were closed, he seemed a handsome corpse.

"He was cheerful, wasn't he, the young master."

In order to answer his servant, the Prince opened his eyes without moving.

"Yes, but it's not the kind of cheer that warms the heart."

BEAUTY
AND
HOLINESS

Ｉｎ ROME, not to dress well is the greatest luxury, and only a few privileged persons can afford it. It's as if an ugly and ill-dressed man didn't even exist. Wherever he might turn he won't find credit, not even to exchange a few words; if he is lucky he will do with a fleeting glance of compassion like the one given to beggars. No matter who he is, such license has not been given even to kings, who have sometimes lost their crowns because they have not been kingly enough. Even in the hours of anguish women will go on talking about the shape of a dress or a hat, of its color, of things liked and desired. Beauty is like another religion.

In the holy city holiness has never excluded beauty, which

it has followed with open interest since the remote times of the pyramids and the sphinx, and kept of them pleasant reminders. In its fight against beauty, holiness was always the one to yield, to wisely find a compromise.

Everything seems to be living for the sake of beauty, from the humblest acts of daily life to the movement of bodies and the customs of clothing. Beauty is the first virtue to be recognized; while Romans talk fleetingly and in low tones about the other virtues, of beauty they can talk without end.

The feeling for beauty is so instinctive, so natural, that its plasticity surprises you while its possessor cannot give you any explanations. He isn't even aware of it, for it's so much his own that he ignores his gift. The young workman sitting at lunch-hour on a step, leaning against a column to eat his bread; or the one who falls asleep while waiting in his truck, as if in sleep he were seeing himself. More than rest he enjoys himself. And he is able to achieve a kind of refinement in slouching. This seems at first to be due to an excessive love of comfort or to lack of respect for others; and yet, as with the Renaissance sculptors—Michelangelo is a good instance—beauty is at the roots of the most relaxed postures. Or take the fashion of wearing his cap made out of a newspaper; the way in which he watches himself, straightens his hair or tie when dressed in Sunday clothes. He stops to look at himself in every mirror on his way; no worry or pain can deprive him of that instant of pleasure he derives from his own body: it's a natural function, like breathing. Mirrors are faithful allies; he would not walk past one without showing eternal gratitude. If there were none, this care and satisfaction would still not lack; he would go like Narcissus to mirror himself in the waters of a fountain or in those of the Tiber.

People's postures lack both stiffness and easy, childish acrobatics. In the warm and colorful light, the sensual air keeps you in a permanent state of inebriation which doesn't affect the brain. From the simplest things to religion, which is also expressed through beauty—churches bathed in light, statues, paintings, music—holiness never intended to divorce beauty, but has been eager to strengthen the union that has been so fruitful to both.

It's clear how Rome could have welcomed the men of the Renaissance: they found its doors open because the Renaissance spirit has always been alive in it; the Florentine movement could not have begun there. Where Christianity had been entrenched, the Renaissance had been an outburst that aimed at the overthrow of the values of life. Rome had not allowed them to be overthrown; between paganism and Christianity it had known how to choose and retain from both. Stringent orders were issued from here against those who wanted to stifle a movement of greatness and health. Rome had never produced weepers, and the monk from Ferrara, Savonarola, would have had to limit himself to caressing the Romans' ears if he had wanted to be heard by them. And Romans love to have their ears caressed, allowing only what they find convenient to enter them. The excesses of the Renaissance were the fault of previous conditions to which it had been a natural reaction, and a reaction to it was the movement that wanted to stifle it: in Florence it is by reaction that things proceed, and after the Renaissance that city kept its medieval character.

The Roman is not excessive, is neither an extremist nor a rebel, he doesn't react; he flaunts his resistance with a method and persistence that at the end resolve the situation in his favor. Rome is a city of balance: foreign extremists call it laziness and indifference, because they fail to understand the great virtue underlying this way of life. When everything seems to fall crashing apart, hidden forms of balance arise from every corner to re-establish order, security and peace. In measure lies the greatness of its civilization, as in measure lay the greatness of the divine Renaissance architects of Florence: in Rome the architects of life had always been of the Renaissance, and extremist views, like waves against rock, have beaten in vain.

NORINA

CHECCO LOOKED upon the Mother Abbess as a very high but familiar authority. Indeed, two times familiar: first, as the eldest daughter of his master, and second, as a highly placed person in that world of which he himself was an active, if not weighty, element; they both worked for the same cause, and after a certain point, as with the soldier under enemy fire, the rank ceases to exist as a moral fact and remains only as a technical necessity. When he used to say: "See you soon, Motherabbess," he greeted someone far above himself yet at the same time one who belonged to him; the ties between him and the nun were so strong that he felt more than at ease with her, he felt bound to her, always ready to treat her with the utmost trust. The same thing was true with a cardinal: in a public ceremony he would kiss his hand with devotion, but if he had to open the door for him on a friendly call to the Prince, he would say with familiar abruptness: "Greetings, Eminence." And that suited the cardinal too, who liked to feel at home on a visit.

Billy-Bet left him absolutely cold. It was as if they didn't exist, or perhaps as if they had been two foreigners who spoke an unknown language. It wasn't that they bothered him, that their sparkling conversation and their musical laughter delivered with perfect timing up and down the scales could irritate him; he didn't hear a word, as if he already knew by heart chapter and verse of what they said. He didn't respond to anything in them, because he found nothing attractive; he had not the least interest or admiration for them or for the events of their life. Such brilliance could not shed light on him; the only pleasurable part of their visit for him was opening the door for them to leave. Their calls were very short and very few, obviously mere formalities. This he could understand, the only thing about them he could understand: they had no time to waste; their days followed a strict, tyrannical schedule. They had to keep giving stealthy glances at their wrists and taking out memo pads from their pockets or purse; one could see right away that they were very busy. Useless is that which keeps one always occupied, without respite.

Whatever Duke Gherardo, or little Dado, the young master, could have said or done—he who had become a man so tall and handsome, so inscrutable and strange, living a thousand leagues away—whatever they could have said about him, he could not but love him. In Checco's soul one of the sublime tenets of the Gospels applied to him, one of those tenets that should be the foundations of it but are, alas, only its peak, a forbidding peak that only a few exceptional men have ever reached, like the high mountain peaks which everybody is content to admire from the foothills: "Thou shalt not pass judgment." He couldn't have passed judgment even within himself, so much he loved him—for him he only felt tenderness. He had loved him when he was a youth and the other an infant. He had taken him in his arms as a newborn, still steaming from the mother's breast, as if he had come out of a pot; holding his breath, he had listened at the Princess' door when she was giving him birth, ready for any order, until the first loud and sure wail reverberated in his heart like a trumpet—the cry of welling life had etched itself into him forever. He had liked to be ordered around by him, the only one who really bossed him in the family, the only one who made him feel the whip of his will. He had never been hurt by him, because deep down he felt loved by that rough and daring boy; his happiness, a happiness that made his heart ache, consisted in spending secretly for him most of the meager salary given him by the boy's father. It's true, reciprocating with a different innocence, Dado had loved Checco more than anyone else in the house, in the first place because he had always served his plans, but also for himself, without any motive or knowing why; he truly loved him in those moments. This Checco felt without knowing. Outwardly so rustic and ignorant of everything, Checco could catch the most delicate, hidden shadings of feeling, could retrieve the least part of it like a grain of gold in the sand. He could seize on the wing the moment born of his love for the child Prince, for the "young master," as he had spontaneously called him. The other didn't resent the name; on the contrary, he seemed to like it. Tenderness for him involved and permeated everything; not loving him he would have been unfaithful to his self.

And Checco felt tenderness for Norina, fourth child and last daughter of His Excellency. He had held her too in his arms right after birth, her flesh more tender than wax; one was afraid of bruising it just by looking. And he had always called her "Little Miss," but since she was not entrusted to his care he had always kept at a respectful distance, so that in meeting her he stood shy and still, as if he had been looking at a very beautiful work of art.

She was still beautiful, and when he ushered the "Little Miss" —now Mrs. Sequi—to the door, the longer she stayed on her visits, that were all supposed to be very short but were always prolonged, the happier he was.

Checco was aware of how much his master loved those visits. To be with Norina was his last mundane joy, his last tie to the world; he would have never let her leave. If he had dared, Checco too would have asked her to stay a little longer; and his face took on new, unknown features, lit by a cheer of which only the memory remained after her departure, a scent in the air. Walking together he scanned her from the top of the head to the point of the little shoes, masterpieces of refined elegance. Her head was a river of gold tumbling over her shoulders; he saw her all made of gold as she crossed the room in front of the papal throne with her very long and straight legs, so narrow at the ankles that one wondered how they could carry her— they didn't seem to belong to a woman; they made you think of pheasants, covered with the gold of their feathers, that strut without touching the ground. "What a beauty," announced Checco's beaming face.

Thirty-five years old, Mrs. Sequi was the mother of three children, two boys and one girl. She had retained the slender and nimble body of her first youth, when she had lived in Via Monserrato, and was from the waist up like a flower on a very long stem. Checco, small and rather ugly as he was, so awkward that one felt sorry for him, had loved beauty in two people: Dado and Norina. Only in those two. People he met elsewhere never touched his imagination, no matter how handsome they were. His eyes could just not be attracted; in a crowd he wouldn't have noticed someone wearing the Tower of Babel on his head. The world of beauty existed for him too, but limited to two persons, Dado and Norina. To some extent they did belong to him also, and on greeting him they both rediscovered the expression of those times when, desiring a favor, they asked the little illiterate peasant for it, without restraint or hesitation. A pity they didn't need anything any more. Although she didn't ask anything of him, Norina would go so far as to do what she wouldn't have done then: once inside the house she slipped her hand under Checco's arm, and very slowly they crossed the immense dark hall, anticipating the hour of peace waiting for her, the serene escape outside her life into the beautiful world of a fairy tale. Checco would have been glad if the hall had been infinitely long, he wouldn't have minded sweeping it once in a while like the squares of Rome, as long as crossing it would have taken more time.

It was she who sent the bottles of wine that Checco hoarded like prizes, drinking a glass from them every day. She sent the cakes, the venison or goose-liver pies on high holidays, prepared by the cook who had the reputation of being the best in Rome; they would have been enough for a dinner of two dozen people, and in Via Monserrato they became a folly, with a slightly offensive tinge: their presence was an affront to everything else, they looked as out of place as if they were things to be hidden or thrown away. Norina knew how they would end, that neither her father nor his servant would touch any of it, that it was the children of the neighboring streets who would enjoy them; she sent them anyway because it amused her, a kind of sweet violence to celebrate a holiday, a still-girlish whim of a youngest daughter. At least master and servant would admire those delicacies, without letting their tastes get involved; they were detached from all vices, even the ones of gluttony, and they preferred that they should be enjoyed by the poor people, for whom they constituted a flight into the land of dreams. The Prince only wanted to see them: he lingered to admire them as one admires pleasing objects in a shop window. He walked around them expressing agreement, until he ordered them to be taken down to the room on the ground floor to be distributed. Checco didn't disdain those delights either; but he didn't feel any desire for them at all, and it never occurred to him to eat any part of it. Only after having given everything away he gathered the crumbs from the tray in the hollow of his hand, and without the shadow of desire among the children sizzling with impatience and voraciousness, he popped them into his mouth—"Goody, goody"—in order to justify their innocent greed. Smiling, he looked over the children who, unable to resist, had begun to bite morsels off their share, or who were devouring theirs with their eyes: "Goody, goody." For a family like the Sequi's, which was opening itself a path to the height of society, an exceptional cook of great fame, of whom everyone likes to talk, is a decisive asset. Nobody refuses invitations when the food is fantastic; gluttony smoothes the way. The vices have a power of attraction that virtues cannot dream of; it seems a paradox yet it's the truth. This the elder Mrs. Sequi knew well: although she wasn't sophisticated—and proud of not being so—she was practical and very intelligent; strong as a lion and smart as a shrew.

They reached the door together and, not needing to announce her, Checco said, beaming:

"Here's the Little Miss."

At these words the Prince sprang to his feet and ran towards his daughter with outstretched arms:

"Come in, my little one . . . ."

Norina entwined her arms tightly around his neck as she used to when she had been a child. They both enjoyed the contact, and they prolonged it, overcoming all reserve and resistance.

"My little darling, it's been so long since I have seen you, you have been away so long, what happened?"

"I was here last week too, Daddy, even if somewhat in a hurry."

"A week without seeing you seems a century."

"What can I do, every day something comes up to wreck my plans."

"But everyone is doing well in your family."

"Yes, Daddy."

Without exception, the Prince's guests were seated facing him on the small leather sofa, which seemed to stand there as a protest against the nice comforts of modern life. It was so hard and bumpy, so thoroughly eviscerated, that after sitting on it a while one's rump would develop callouses; so narrow that two people who were a little bulky would have had difficulty sitting together. And once seated the problem would have been to get them out. Luckily father and daughter were equally slender, so the Prince could sit next to her—only with her did he do so, happy because of the closeness that made him feel like one of two souls living in the heart of a fruit. Once in a while Norina leaned her head on his shoulder, flooding it with her hair, and the old man dipped his hand in that golden softness, never tired of feeling it run between his fingers.

"My own, my little darling."

When Norina left, she had to comb herself as if she were coming out of a tryst, and without a mirror in the whole house —nobody ever noticed this lack except Norina, who had so often repeated in vain:

"Oh, Father, not even a mirror left in this house anymore," words that were like seeds falling on stone, on concrete.

"What would we use a mirror for?"

"I could use one, don't I count for anything? I am not an old woman yet."

"You carry a mirror in your purse."

"Yes, but that's too tiny, I need something else when I am so untidy. First you ruffle all my hair and then you don't give me a chance to rearrange it."

The Prince, quite cheerful, would call out loudly:

"Checco! Checco! Get your shaving mirror for Norina."

"Good thing there's still Checco with a little coquetry."

Checco would bring the mirror. If there was still daylight they went under the window, where he held it while Norina made untold efforts to be able to see herself, Checco's face beaming in front of her: "How pretty she is." If there wasn't any light, they went next to the lamp on the desk: a hopeless affair, and Norina ended up by losing her patience.

"Well; no mirror, no light, nothing: this is the most wretched house in the world. When Mother was alive it wasn't like this."

"Then there was a woman . . . but now I'm alone."

"Why do things have to be this way if you are alone?"

"Is it really true? There isn't anything in this house?" asked the Prince, moving closer as she finished rearranging her hair.

"There is you, Daddy, the most beautiful thing that one can wish, the most beautiful thing I know. Only you should keep up a little with the times, you live too much in history."

"But I do keep up, you know, I really do."

"I know, I know, but even unimportant things, trivial if you wish, after a certain point become a necessity."

After all the suffering she would be ready, more or less. On that day Norina was thoughtful, slightly worried:

"Father, I came to bother you. You already know what it's about before I open my mouth: the usual thing. I know how much you dislike it but I know you are doing it for my sake, you have never declined and this shows enough the greatness of your love. I wish I could spare you, but peaceful coexistence with my mother-in-law is at stake. Once she said: 'The Princess came into our house with only the shirt on her back.' "

"And what did you answer?"

"She didn't say it to me, but to someone who took pains to let me know. Ha! If she were to tell me, I have a ready answer: 'It's a pity, dear lady, that I didn't have a handkerchief to match, so I could cover my nose and keep out the ghastly smell of sausage floating through your house!' "

"But your father-in-law does like you."

"Yes, Father, he is good, he is really good and likes me. After all, she does too, but you know, with men it's easy to be on friendly terms, with women it's different."

Norina used to invite her father two or three times a year—four in cases of emergency—to a reception of the great, given by her in-laws, with that lavishness the new rich wield to challenge the criticism and penuriousness of the old. These parties were games bristling with difficulty for the hostess, who didn't spare fireworks when introducing him to the guests: "His Excellency, the Prince of Santo Stefano, father of my daughter-in-law," and would add for the benefit of novices and foreigners: "Secret Chamberlain to His Holiness." To a woman of such practical character, so blunt in words and deeds, blunt to the point of seriously embarrassing her interlocutors, who would find themselves suddenly in a corner without hope of retreat, such an introduction didn't seem too long: on the contrary, if it had to be drawn out for half an hour she would have stayed sweet and submissive, ready to go on with it for a whole week. It made her forget the shortness of her own: Pia Sequi. Could such a strong and important woman, head of a business network and of one of the richest Roman families (some said the richest), be satisfied with so short a name, so meaningless, full of wind, made of nothing, slippery, which when pronounced would run out of the mouth instead of filling it? Once she had had a maid called Teodolinda Cacciadragoni; every time the maid's name came up, Mrs. Sequi became uneasy, nervous, mean. Could a lady called Pia Sequi and nothing more have a maid with the name of Teodolinda Cacciadragoni? And as the perfidious maid had discovered her lady's soft spot, she found a thousand ways to flaunt it. So she was fired. Except for this weakness—and who doesn't have one?—she had a heart big as a house. She was generous by nature, and no one who went to ask her help returned empty-handed; she sincerely hated poverty and the very thought of it was enough to soften and at the same time irritate her, she felt it to be something against everybody and against herself. She would have liked to have a magic wand so that all could be as rich as herself, that no one should suffer any deprivation. To those who would describe to her someone's troubles and ask for assistance, she used to answer "Dammit!" She said it so well, with a voice coming from the heart, that she was known in Roman society simply as "Dammit."

At one time Mrs. Sequi had to close a rather important business deal with a diminutive little man who had a voice like a thread of silk. After making her position clear in a few well-chosen words, she listened to that of the other, which didn't coincide with hers at all. She tried to meet him half-way, to make him reconsider, but without success. Four times the little man repeated his speech gently and slowly, changing every word but arriving at the same conclusion. Mrs. Sequi, with bulging eyes and hands on her waist, raised herself from the sofa and yelled: "Stick it up your ... !" The little man stood up too, his eyes as hermetically closed as if they had never been open, his head lost between the shoulders, whence came a voice very much thinner than that of a mosquito: "I accept your conditions, my lady." Another time, on a horrid winter day, she was bedded with a cold when some French diplomats of the kind who are always saying *"Exquis, adorable, amiable, ravissant"* were expected for lunch. The date couldn't be changed, nor did she want to miss it. When she was ill, even if with a slight seasonal chill, she lapsed into that state of purified animal fright that the strong and the simple experience facing an evil with which they have no familiarity. She came downstairs in very bad humor and a few degrees of fever, wrapped in a fur coat. During the meal the wind made a loose jalousie rattle on one of the windows. A butler serving at the table turned towards the window with the intention of opening it. Guessing his thought, she stopped him with a whoop: "Young man, I will kick you in the balls if you open that window!"

"You are giving a ball?"

"No, Daddy, a twenty-four person dinner next Thursday. I came to tell you early so that you can prepare yourself for the sacrifice. It will be a dinner for the usual friends, plus a big financier. Mother-in-law doesn't forget business for the sake of society. They aren't people whom you'll like to be with, Daddy."

"It doesn't matter."

"But you do so well for Mother-in-law, and she would blame me for your absence. She won't have peace unless they put a crown on her head. I would like to make one out of cardboard and shove her head into it. During the war she had set the idea aside, now she is at it with all her might—but it doesn't seem she'll have success."

"Tell your mother-in-law not to forsake charity and she will get what she wants. One has to make use of human frailty; without it people would be too beautiful, pure beauty frightens them, they are satisfied to be that only half-way."

"You know, Daddy, how much she gives and in so many

ways, she really loves the poor, everyone knows it. She may have many faults, but not this."

"Well, she will get it, you can be sure of it. I know that your mother-in-law doesn't have the avarice of the rich, that she has kept the generosity of her laborer's heart. I will come to your dinner, and it won't be a bother—it will be such a light task if it will help my little one."

"Thank you, Daddy, very much. And now to change the subject completely: have you seen Gherardo?"

"Yes."

"He told me. He called on you, and of course he told you what he told me."

"Right."

"He's getting married."

"And he is already sorry before even going through with it. He tastes the bitter pleasure of setting himself against his own self, not to mention others."

Norina was puzzled.

"Alberto and my in-laws have said a hundred times that they were ready to offer him a job in their enterprises; something that would be worthy of his name, and still leave him personal autonomy and all the freedom he wants."

"But he doesn't want to take money from them, this is the mistake he is making. He doesn't want a job with the Sequis."

"And he does take it from that kind of a woman?"

"Once on the evil track, he takes pleasure in walking on it to the end. Gherardo is the first one to condemn what he says and what he does. His bitterness is caused by a misunderstanding in which he fell, a deep and real one: your brother is a vessel overflowing with bitterness. I have never given thought to money, and this is a fault in your brother's eyes. As far as I am concerned money doesn't exist and never did, one needs so little of it to live on, almost nothing. I could live on less, and then I would feel even happier and more proud of myself. The error of our times consists in the belief that happiness follows money, when a few cents a day are enough for happiness, if you have a treasure inside the soul. And the fewer the cents, the greater the happiness, the higher, the more dazzling. Whoever looks for happiness in money is on the wrong path, and who thinks to save his soul through money is more wrong yet: it is through money that one loses it."

"Now listen, Daddy, I don't like poverty either and you know it, I never did like it. Isn't it strange, I am your daughter, yet I am not made for poverty: its very thought fills me with sadness. I can only feel sorry for the poor, they make me truly suffer, and I give them as much as I can because I understand their suffering."

"I only tried to make him see the error that constrains him. A hopeless task, since he knows it better than I do. The job offered by his in-laws doesn't soil his honor, and nobody prevented him from looking for something else. But it's dishonorable to accept money, under any condition, from a woman like his. Gherardo is going through a stage of rebellion—beyond the distraction that is in all hearts in these difficult times of ours, he suffers that of his special situation. Your mother had been in want just as I am, and we were happy together. We came to know the total joy which the union of two beings, if true, can give."

"Daddy, Mother was a woman of a strange constitution: she made herself a dress once in three years, and she wore the same dress to go out in her whole life."

"And she was so beautiful in that effacement which emphasized her nobility: the most beautiful and graceful in Rome."

"You two were certainly made for each other, inch for inch. You had been clever in choosing her, in having found her. Poor Daddy, today you couldn't find one like her, people like you have become extinct, they have disappeared from the face of the earth."

"There always are, there always have been and will be: in such numbers that you can't even imagine, infinitely more than what you believe or think. If it weren't true, you wouldn't be here talking with your father."

"Today theories and reasoning don't count any more, everyone wants to have a good time, because one lives only once."

"And you call it a good time, this blind, dumb struggle that destroys mankind from the highest rung to the lowest? You call it a good time, to fall under the power of a prostitute for the love of money? Gherardo will become aware of all the implications as soon as he will find himself alone with his shame."

"It seems she's very beautiful. Gherardo told me he had been madly in love with her, perhaps he still is."

"But how can he imagine himself next to her? The accounts don't balance on either side, and it will be obvious in every action of their life together. He puts himself at the service of this woman who is marrying him because she is caught by the whim of becoming a princess. A whim such as women of her kind get—cold, ambitious, certainly evil. She hopes to become a lady, but when she realizes that she has merely chased a ghost, she will turn all her malice on him."

"Let's be honest, Daddy, how has Gherardo supported himself during the fifteen years he's been away? You couldn't send money to him because you didn't have any."

"At first he asked for it, and I sent him what I could."

"Which surely must have been nothing as far as he was concerned."

"I sent what I could. Then he stopped asking, he didn't write any longer. A few short greetings, two words to tell me he was well in all respects."

113

"He asked me for money at the beginning, too, but only once and in great secrecy. He didn't want my husband to find out about it; and as I didn't have cash available right then, I had to make a deal with our jeweler. After that nothing. How did he live those fifteen years? Does he work? Does he have a profession? Which? It doesn't look like he has any. You can well say that one should forget money, but after a while it will remind you of itself and force you to think about it. As you must have seen, Gherardo doesn't look like a man in straits, but like one who lives a life of ease which lacks nothing."

The Prince riveted his eyes on the worn and scuffled floor of the room, where he seemed to discover the chasms opened by his children: he began talking to himself.

"Money is the great misunderstanding of our times, the enemy of man: I won't get tired of repeating it. Every ill proceeds from it, it's the only cause of unhappiness and misfortune, in everyone. To have it or to have it not is the same; different causes of the same unhappiness. Money never mattered to me, the less I had of it the happier I was: light, peaceful; the less my day cost, the more beautiful, heavenly it was, and the more worthy I felt of my status. And when I found myself alone and banished everything from around me, it was as if my body grew wings. Now that my day doesn't cost anything —a few crumbs for myself and this good creature who is with me—and no things clutter around me, I feel myself close to a dazzling peak of light and beauty: the highest, unalterable, intangible, eternal conquest. And my children come to talk to me about money. How can they be so blind as not to distinguish reality before their eyes? Those whom I created, raised and taught in this house."

"I haven't married Alberto because of his money, you know that. Mine was a romantic marriage, not one of interest or convenience."

"Yes, you were lucky; both such beautiful children, such a handsome couple."

"I was in love with Alberto as only a girl who is in love for the first time can be. Alberto has been my first and only love. I was in love with him but not the way you mean it; when I say 'love' you don't understand me, I am sure."

"Why shouldn't I understand you?"

"No, Daddy, I am sure of it. We speak the same language but this word has different meanings for us. I like my husband," Mrs. Sequi said in a clear, crisp voice.

"Of course you like him, and you think I don't understand? You like him, it was the reason for having chosen him; it's the way it should be, you would be wretched if you didn't."

"I like him today as the day that I married him, as when we were betrothed. I like him now as when I looked at him and we were only friends, aching inside from the desire of belonging to him, that he may be mine, and I his. Daddy, after fifteen years I like my husband as I did then—even more. I like everything about him, the way he moves his eyes, the way he walks, his poise. The way he talks and the way he gets in and out of the car, the way he drives it: there isn't one moment in his life that could move me to judge or criticize him, there isn't a thing that I don't like in his person, or a space between us, a point of coldness. I like everything, and everything brings out only desire in me—after fifteen years I am not sated of him; I want him!" she said with her voice raised to a compelling tone: "Do you see, now?"

The last statement seemed to bewilder the Prince, who had followed his daughter's spiraling speech, moving closer in a suggestion of understanding agreement. He stopped short, watching her.

"In this liking," Norina went on in a normal conversational tone, "in this liking money plays a certain role, too, not a small

115

role either, its action takes place stage center. It's in his middle-class foundations, with the overtones of a working-man born and raised in wealth. He has his mother's blood, bringing sureness to his actions, the habits of a gentleman not worn down by too long use, by habit and by that feeling of satiety which dulls the drive or takes away most of its taste. In him there is still the curiosity and greed of his origins, a quickness that ancient nobles have lost; they who are not aware of what they do, for having done it so often, who reach a mechanical formality after which they think everything is due to them, who are not attracted to anything. There is nothing mechanical about him, nor is there any sign of the effort which can be read so clearly on his parents' brows, and which often darkens theirs; his face never clouds over for any reason, nothing can disturb its calm. He has arrived from the start yet keeps the vigor of recent conquest, without having known the hardships of the eve. Dear Daddy, there is more joy in red blood than in blue. Alberto knows this joy."

The Prince seemed to be searching for a foothold on a path that had turned out to be unsure.

"But you are happy with your husband."

"No, Daddy, I never told you this so clearly before, I am not happy with my husband. This is just the reason why I am not happy with him: because I like him, because I like him so much, because I always have liked him, and still do."

"Alberto loves you."

"After his fashion, yes. Which isn't exactly yours or mine. I am his wife and mother of his children. One day we will be at the head of his family. He used to like me and he still doesn't dislike me, he hasn't thrown me in a corner nor does he brush me off, he doesn't despise me. He is still my husband and a sound one when he does remember, sometimes he does remember me, but very seldom, and I am too proud to remind

116

him. This doesn't prevent him from going with every woman who happens to come his way, he has done it always. I can't be sure of the exact date, but I know Alberto gave in to the first adventure a few months after our wedding. I understood this only later, at the time I didn't. And yet he isn't a skirt-chaser, he doesn't run after them, he isn't morbidly obsessed; on the contrary, he is extremely calm in his actions, smiling, serene, very youthful. Being rich, with a happy body exercised in every way since childhood, worldly, women fall for him in numbers that would make one's head spin; but his head is so well organized that it doesn't spin, doesn't get unbalanced—however, when he likes a woman he isn't going to let her go to waste. He never had a real, lasting relationship; in general his affairs fizzle quickly, sometimes after a few sittings, from what I understand some even after just one. I am aware of what happens, I am not as silly as when I left this house. He thinks of it as a duty to his sex, a point of honor, of virility. Can one say no to a woman when she is pleasing, or, indeed, beautiful? These are things that need to be satisfied, as at certain times of the day one eats or sleeps. And the women, besides the pleasure they get from his body, enjoy the spite they are doing me."

The Prince raised his head with an effort of will, after having kept it bent during a period of discouragement.

"Alberto is still young...he is only a year older than you are."

"I am not an old woman either, and I could have as many men as I wished."

"Don't say that, Norina, I don't want you to say such things: it is blasphemy."

But Norina went on talking to herself.

"My name—I'm rich—still young and pretty—I only have the embarrassment of choice."

"I forbid you to say such words in my presence. In your husband's case, such behavior is flighty and shallow, certainly to be disapproved; but in yours it would be a fault for which there is no forgiveness, one that would cleave in your soul a furrow that no repentance, no regret could erase; a pain hidden within yourself that would harrow the rest of your life."

"Ha, Ha! Didn't I tell you, Daddy, that we talk the same language without being able to understand each other?"

"You only have to increase your care, your affection for him and your children, increase your goodness: he will return wholly to you when the vigor of his youth with its regrettable excesses will have passed. Then it will be he who will suffer from his behavior. Your virtue will give you back all his heart, repentant; he will acknowledge having done wrong and will love you more and better than he ever did. Your beauty will be enlarged a hundred times in his eyes, virtue will give you a new beauty, one that won't fade; he will recognize that you had been the true, only woman for him—the others he won't even recall, and if sometimes the thought forces him to remember, it will be only to despise them, to see their ugliness together with his own."

"Yes, yes . . . on the one hand, he can act in perfect freedom, and I, on the other, wait till he is bored by his amusement. And once I am old, I have nothing else left to do but bite my fingers for not being able to take revenge. No thanks, dear Daddy."

"A man's actions do not have the same weight, the same responsibility."

"What my husband does is not done with men of little weight and responsibility, but with women, and usually with married ones."

"If there are wicked women in this world it doesn't mean that you have to bespatter yourself with the same wickedness."

"Ha, Ha! This time I really made up my mind, my husband will get what he deserves. A husband isn't real, he isn't a husband until he is cuckolded. I can assure you that mine will be, too."

"I know you are saying this to suggest your disappointment, to release your pain, and I understand it very well; but I am certain you will never do it."

"I will do it, that's for sure, as soon as I can. The funny thing is I will do it coldly, without desire."

"You are talking now like one who is insane, without being able to judge the import of your words."

"What import? When my husband will know about it, he will be the first to recognize its fairness. Perhaps he is wondering why I haven't done it before now, or he thinks that I must have acted so carefully and discreetly that nothing transpired."

"Your husband cannot be as degenerate or insane as you seem to be now."

"I tell you, I will do it. And without even having the satisfaction of seeing him displeased, angry, indignant; otherwise I would have done it long ago."

"Tomorrow go to your confessor and tell him what you told me."

"No, I won't, I will go to him afterwards; besides, you are my confessor."

"I forbid you to utter heresies in this house."

"Anyway, you will be the first one to know about it."

"Then I will chase you out, and never again open the door to you."

"Why do you want a tragedy at all costs, Daddy? This is a comic scene, a bedroom farce."

The Prince, after having reflected on his daughter's words rather than having listened to them, seemed to have drawn his conclusions. Holding her hand, he began to speak almost with sweetness:

"My little one, you wish that your man were all for your-self alone. You have every reason and right to do so, it would be wonderful if he could understand it, but his shallowness prevents him from being able to tell the gold from the tinsel. You will help him know the true greatness and beauty of life, you will prepare him this unknown joy. You would like to live with him as your father and mother lived together. In their minds thoughts of this kind could not have occurred even in dreams, or as a joke. Their minds were built so that arguments of such a nature could not be harbored in them. You are like your parents: death could not break their love, their faithful-ness, their purity. When your mother died I wasn't old yet, I was less than fifty, but never for a moment did I think of having another woman; we stayed united as on the day we were bound by the priest. My love for your mother is still a flame that lights every action of the day, your mother is still with me as she was when she walked these floors. She was an angel already then. What divides us now is only a short interval in which I have to deepen the purity of my love. My love for her was not pure enough, not beautiful enough; that is why the Lord has wanted to inflict such a sacrifice on me, so that my love may become deeper, more pure, more beautiful."

Norina seemed to be daydreaming.

"Perhaps it's true that I am like you. It's true, Daddy, this is my problem, this is what makes me suffer; because everybody is so very different."

"So you too have something to blame on me, you too have come here to blame your poor father. Some days ago your brother called to offend and ridicule what is sacred in me, the supreme beauty of life, my faith and my poverty; today you come to reproach me for the virtue that your mother and I have passed on to our daughter. Norina, forget what you told me in a moment of lost, hopeless hatred. Do believe your father, he is telling the truth—beyond my words are lies and infamy."

"I can only repeat my final decision, ripened to exhaustion: one of these days your daughter will go with a man who is not her husband, wherever and whichever way he wishes. And afterwards she will come to give you an account of it, and you will see that it isn't as serious as you think."

"Go away! Go away!" The Prince walked away from her, moving his arms as if to chase her: "Go away! Run to your husband, run to embrace your children and you will find yourself again, because now you are lost."

DINNER
AT NINE,
DAMMIT!

T HE TRAFFIC in and out the Santo Stefano Palace, which would have tickled a writer's imagination, didn't interest in the least anyone else on Via Monserrato. No one looked twice at the passage of the extremely tall and thin, slightly bent old man—a tent pole—followed at the heels by a small round man—a little barrel—reaching half-way between the elbow and the shoulder of the first. They passed in full darkness during the winter, regardless of the weather: both in similar and always the same tight little over-coats; or in always identical all-black suits which by now were all one with the bodies, like a varnish. The first lights of the day in spring and fall, or the full sunlight in summer, brought in relief the antiquity of their bodies and clothes—things that the street urchins had seen among the first sights of their lives, and now were being seen the same way by their sons. No one looked at them and if they were noticed it was in the way one sees the sun passing over the edge of the roof, over the neighbor's windows; or as the falling of rain is seen upon opening a window in the morning. No one watched the coming and going of the little man with the round pink face on which there seemed to be imprinted a smile, who carried a canvas satchel folded under his arm at noon, and came back half an hour later carrying the same bag seemingly still empty. Or the idling of a huge, somber car, weighted with solemnity, and the plates "SCV"—Holy City of the Vatican—until the extremely tall old man appeared, displaying legs like sticks inside black silk hose and silver-clasped pumps, the breeches ballooning at the thighs that emphasized the leanness instead of hiding it, the sleeves and breast all ruffles bordered with gold galloons, a sword at his side and a cape from shoulders to waist forming butterfly wings; around the neck a great white collar with a hundred pleats in which his face seemed to drown. On his head a beret surmounted by the parabola of a white ostrich feather. In this dress Don Filippo di Santo Stefano reached an astounding height, from which the equine face radiated the icy haughtiness of certain Renaissance paintings that make one stop abruptly and speechless in museums. When he appeared in the doorway, the "Heavenly Woman," who had been anxiously waiting for half an hour, ran to him with her eyes lifted to the sky, ran right and left, ahead and behind, until he stepped into the car. Always present and always the same, the little man followed without missing a step. Or, some afternoon at that gate on which the dust of ages rested in layers, one of those cream or pea-colored cars would be waiting, a mile long and shiny as a mirror, the latest great work of the world's most renowned factory; standard appliance of American and Russian embassies, plus a few people blessed by the seductive fame of money. Two or three times a year the same car, as if on oil, would slide up to that door around nine o'clock waiting for the tall and lean man to come out, with the small round one hiding behind him; both were unchanged in expression or in dress from when they had left for Mass at dawn. This last unusual exit the Prince would have gladly refused, if it hadn't involved the happiness of his tenderly beloved daughter. Events that the inhabitants of Via Monserrato saw without noticing, as one sees the strands of rain or the rays of the sun.

The invitations read: "Dinner at nine." Everyone who read it added: "Dammit!"

The Sequis' villa in the new Monti Parioli district, although grandiose, had a markedly middle-class character. Mrs. Pia Sequi was biding her time, and had for a long time earmarked a historic palace for the long awaited day in which a countess' crown would fall on her head. An event which she certainly did her best to precipitate: the short and skippery name would be enriched by a well-turned-out pedestal. Mrs. Pia Sequi was one thing, Countess Sequi something else—not counting the possibility of some further addition to it, who knows from where. Anyway, her middle-class villa was grandiose, and above all, comfortable: being from northern Italy she made haste to surround herself with the wonderful conquests achieved in this field by modern science. In her kitchens and laundries all the appliances were the latest products that electrical engineering had perfected, and they were objects of admiration in the whole town. The machinery of the house was even more famous than its reception wing, in which Titian and Veronese, Canaletto, Bronzino and Giambologna were well displayed.

"Dinner at nine" read the invitations, and "Dinner at nine," she herself told at full voice those directly invited. "Dammit," they said or thought, depending on the situation. She informed the guests as she led them through the house: "Until midnight we eat in the dining room, where the conversation will be centralized; afterwards when there will be more of us, conversation will be decentralized," and she showed the other room, a glass-enclosed gallery built over a terrace, replete in every season with exotic plants and beautiful rare flowers that conjured a paradisiacal vision. These were the tournaments over which Mrs. Sequi liked to preside, putting all her strength to service; not even the old Prince of Santo Stefano would resist her call. An invitation extended to more than a dozen guests at the Sequis might include up to fifty; the rare formal dinners were given with the utmost splendor, and not without a hidden ulterior motive.

During these special occasions the Prince of Santo Stefano used to sit in the clothes he had served Mass in, a stiff collar and a faded, somewhat greasy black tie, at the right hand of the hostess; the place was his, first because of his title, then his age, his honorary position with the Supreme Pontiff, not to mention a bottomless reserve of other honorifics and decorations. Mrs. Sequi had not yet come by the opportunity to relegate him to second place. Only another Roman prince with a higher position than his could have supplanted him, or a prince of the Church. Neither the two or three Roman nobles who had these prerequisites nor a cardinal had ever climbed her stairs. Cardinals, even the more worldly ones whom one can easily meet around the tables of foremost patricians, are notoriously wary of accepting invitations to houses where splendor and wealth still smell of varnish; so that the place of honor, at least for the moment, was due to the man who looked like the beggar of the party.

That evening Mrs. Sequi had at her left a well-known banker, the most renowned in Italy. If her right represented the decorative part of life, the importance of which she didn't deny even while giving it short shrift, the left stood for what was solid, the part she knew and appreciated more than any other. She was a woman who always knew how to keep life's values in balance. Four gilt chandeliers stood guard over the table; the quivering flames of their hundred candles, multiplied to infinity by mirrors everywhere, created a starburst that expanded beyond walls and ceilings to merge with the air. The gilded silverware framed ancient and famous beflowered porcelain settings that had come from Saxony by way of Russia. Cross-cut crystals spread diamond rays over gold and flowers, over the general pleasantness.

Turned towards his neighbor without bending his body, as if he were talking in an opposite direction, with a stiffness that could have been either offensive or defensive, the Prince spoke, with a voice that seemed to be issuing from a man of iron or stone:

"The more one finds himself in an exalted position, the more he ought to be concerned with others, till he achieves complete self-oblivion. Only the poor have a right to be concerned with their own selves, even if they do it the whole day long. Unless it's Sunday, which is reserved for the Lord to Whom all should consecrate their labors, and the poor, their material sufferings, which one day the Lord will transform into rejoicing. No one will be as happy as the poor on that day of feasting: they will be the chosen, the Lord's favorites; they will be loved by the Lord, who will be generous in His favors, in the gifts He will freely bestow just as He will be stern with the wealthy and pitiless with the miser; on that day the poor will feel richer and more secure than a king. To be concerned with others till we forget ourselves. When we cease to notice our physical being we have reached the sublime goal. This rising above the frail and deceptive burden that is our human body, this transformation

126

of everything into spirit, shall give us a light-headed feeling, so great is the height we shall have reached on granitic foundations. For us to gain the place destined by the Lord, our life has to become a mission, an example in its every action, in every moment of the day."

Raising her head towards the glass panes of the ceiling Mrs. Sequi opened her arms:

"What winged words! Not one wrinkle in them. Sublime expressions, Excellency, that seem to descend from Heaven rather than rise from a table where people are eating." Then, lowering her tone by three-fourths: "Their practical application, however, is another matter."

The Prince gazed at her sternly.

"First of all I should point out to you that it is by my own effort that I reached an exalted position; second of all, if I don't begin by being concerned with my own business, how can I be concerned about other people? I too would become like the poor who wait for the Lord's generosity; we would be like two blind men in the same ditch. It is by being concerned with myself that I will have something to give the poor."

"It is not enough to give away surplus. One has to give with the heart, not because of duty or convenience."

"Slowly, just a moment: I try to give whatever I can, and that with my whole heart and soul; but it is obvious that the first share is mine. The larger mine is, the more I can give others. You don't expect me to rack my brains and eat gruel so that I can give everything to them; if I get a nervous breakdown I won't be any good either to me or to them. My father used to work, and how: he worked at night too, and didn't rest even on Sundays. The Lord must have forgiven him, working is not a sin, sin is to be without doing anything. I am just like him, his exact image, I can't stand still a second; when it seems I am resting is the time that I work hardest, I work with the brain, my head is a construction yard. Let the others do as I do; so far as I am concerned, the idea of going without food in order to give to those who sleep hoping for carrots to fall in their mouths is something that, to tell you the truth, I cannot stomach."

"We shouldn't be thinking about ourselves, our life is a mission."

"My mission is to take care of my son, my grandchildren, and all those who live or work around me; then to be concerned also about the sons and grandchildren of others—but mine come first. Have you ever seen a mother hen? She rustles from morning to night, but for her chicks."

"The hen is an animal."

"Exactly, after having made life too artificial we have to start back at the origins and learn something from the animals who live truth. Animals are pure and we aren't."

Turning to her left-hand neighbor:

"And what is . . . your mission?"

The renowned financier, who had eavesdropped on the conversation, looked at her in surprise, his glance answering with a question: "Don't you know?" Then he laughed with false modesty:

"My mission is to exploit the market."

Jumping on her chair, Mrs. Sequi dropped the spoon which almost broke the saucer, and clapped her hands together. Everybody turned towards her.

"Here is a dynamic word: the market. Just to hear it I feel tingling all over. To have the market on your fingertips, to close deals from morning to night, to make the fair and foul weather on the exchange, to create activity from nothing; new enterprises, industries, to dream up traffic that brings well-being to thousands of people: This is life's mission."

"You too know how to draw a bargain, and from what I un-

128

derstand quite shrewdly," he said, looking around instinctively.

"Oh, they don't amount to anything, what can you expect? I am a woman, a housewife; I swim in a glass of water and I would like to sail the ocean." She lowered her voice, leaning her head towards the banker's. "As soon as we are alone I will tell you about some plans I have."

"I am at your service, my lady."

At Mr. Sequi's right sat the old Princess Del Balzo, whose undying attachment to the monarchy was legendary.

"Every time I pass in front of those gates, I close my eyes, I begin to cry, it's so sad. I keep telling my chauffeur to take a detour but he does everything to drive by the palace whenever I don't pay attention; he must be a republican."

"Maybe he is shy or afraid they'll think him subversive."

"Nonsense, he swears to be a dyed-in-the-wool monarchist, but I don't believe him and have good reasons for doubt. Who knows what he does when he gets that ballot in his hands? Subversive, indeed . . . so I am a subversive."

Mr. Sequi laughed good-naturedly.

"It's the others who tried to subvert me, but they haven't succeeded. They won't even on the guillotine. To think that they placed a civil servant where a crowned man should stand. An anchor-point, like the sun, to whom one can turn for faith and counsel. From that time I suffer of spells of dizziness, it's like living on a merry-go-round. To have banished royalty, that greatest and most beautiful thing, from the surface of the earth. The few shaggy kings that are still around pretend not to be themselves, they live like everybody else, they try to mix with the crowd." The Princess closed her eyes, "The world is a wreck."

And on the left Marchioness Genoveffa Terribili, three times widowed, twice marchioness and twice countess: the fiercest woman in Rome. Mrs. Sequi used to tell her with a sigh:

"Well, my dear Genoveffa; some have it, some don't." They understood each other perfectly.

After her third husband had died, Marchioness Terribili had not settled down into a new marriage. She instead had closed up shop and had become a rabid feminist. She dedicated herself completely to the emancipation and organization of women. At the headquarters of her association she made speeches of a fanaticism so extreme that the most exasperated politician wouldn't dream of making them.

"Dear friend, the world will always be a brier, an inferno, unless leadership will pass into women's hands."

She quoted the bees as the example of a perfect community.

Mr. Sequi amused himself vastly with her: "Did you by any chance deal with your husbands as bees do?"

"At that time I didn't know how the bees operated, which is a pity because they would have deserved it, my husbands. England's great historical periods were due to two women: Elizabeth and Victoria, Russia's to Catherine, Catherine de Medici in France, Isabella in Spain, Maria Teresa in Austria. . . ."

"It isn't possible that these excellent ladies had at their sides some representative of the other sex who at the right moment would whisper in their ears a good suggestion?"

"It isn't true, it's false, a lie, an infamy!" shouted Marchioness Terribili, "and even if it were true they would still remain great, it means that women know how to choose their assistants with an intuition alien to men. A man in their place would have called a madman to his side, and ruined everything. Joan of Arc! Catherine Sforza! Saint Catherine of Siena! Cristina of Sweden. . . ."

"Slowly, don't go so fast, otherwise your list will run out too soon. I won't bother you with mine, it would keep you listening for a week."

"Of course, because you have the upper hand, you exploit and usurp your position, defend it tooth and nail and won't let women pass."

"Could a woman have built Saint Peter's dome?"

"Much better. She would have made it larger and much more beautiful."

"Yet it was built by a man."

"And therefore it's gray, flat, undistinguished. Anyway, women are always trapped by men."

"But you fell three times in that trap without getting hurt."

"I have a right to speak, I have had experience."

"It's funny, I always thought that men used to fall into traps."

"Not in the least."

"Yet women are more trap-shaped. Or perhaps they fall together."

"Men will have to be replaced everywhere."

"Will the Pope have to be a woman too?"

"He first of all."

"But there will always be a time when you need us."

"Not at all, your contribution is minimal, insignificant; all it takes is to analyze the fluid and reproduce it chemically."

"But wouldn't it be easier for you to take it from its rightful source?"

Mrs. Sequi, facing her, smiled: "Genoveffa, how is my husband behaving?"

"Not too bad, considering what he is, but his sex is all wrong."

"Don't be too hard on him, he is a fine boy."

Alberto Sequi had Leonia Macuto at his side: she was the woman of the day. On Via Veneto there were riots at her passage. Brown beauty with the paleness of a magnolia, the most unsettling and mysterious. She had appeared on the skies of Rome like a shooting star. Who was she? Where did she come from? All her personality suggested warm origins: the Middle East? Greece? South America? Mexico? Spain? Would she stay in Rome? How long? Where would she go if she left? Was she single or did she have a husband? In what part of the globe? She spoke Italian well with a foreign accent that was impossible to pinpoint. Without her having to show an identity card her feminine glamor and the richness of her clothes had opened many doors wide. With the secret hope that she would decide to open one of her own. Nothing. Much gossip but not a shred of evidence. She had on a dress with a décolletage that made her seem nude from the waist up. Alberto Sequi and she began to tease each other; excellent beginnings between a man and a woman. In fact he was the only man for whom Leonia showed an interest or at least some curiosity, in spite of the teasing. For the others she had only icy indifference. And she seemed a very warm woman.

"A woman ought to show something, that we know. It has always been done and will always be done—it's an institution. But by showing everything as you are doing now, you will only get the opposite effect."

"Are you sure?"

"Yes, on this subject I am a reactionary fuddy-duddy." He went on brushing her ear with his words: "What's left for the man you love? No surprises."

"A woman may show everything and still keep some surprises for her man." She appeared to be making fun of him.

"I wait for that surprise with closed eyes—darkness is even better."

"And when the man of whom you were speaking does not exist, I think it's very generous of a woman to show as much as possible. You must be awfully selfish." It was hard to interpret the stare she turned on Alberto Sequi.

Billy-Bet, although seated very far from each other, had found a way to display their exemplary union that defied any distance:

"Ha, ha! Ha, ha!"

Indeed, the farther they were the better it came out:

"Ha, ha! Ha, ha!"

On the left of Alberto Sequi sat the young Countess Rossellino, a divorcée—notwithstanding the fact that divorce is not recognized in Italy. She relished making the most pointless and esoteric remarks in her conversation, without any attempt at continuity. She had lived six months with her husband, claimed to have had enough of it, and now believed in so doing to have broken some kind of a record.

"It's easy to see that man has learned to fly from the birds. . . ."

At these words, Alberto Sequi shifted to her his attention previously monopolized by his right-hand neighbor.

"Therefore airplanes should look exactly like birds, yet they are very much like fish. It looks like the air is full of fish."

"So you do find a great difference between birds and fish?"

The young countess stared at him with an exaggerated scowl.

"I could prove it to you myself that the difference is only an illusion."

"This conversation will have to stop for reasons of censorship."

"But could be continued in another room, where jurisdiction applies."

"Ha, ha! Ha, ha!"

Norina was surrounded by two of the most boring people in the city. General Lauriti told anecdotes more than half a century old, about when he had been a young artillery lieutenant at the war games in the Aosta Valley. It seems that all the officers had been invited by Queen Margherita, who was vacationing there. They had replied to the unexpected invitation by letting the sovereign know that they were just then returning from field exercises, so that it would have taken some time for them to spruce up and change uniforms. The Queen answered that they should come over just as they were, she would be even more glad to see them in fatigues.

"What a woman!" concluded the General. "She could deal with every kind of people without losing an ounce of her royalty."

"Is that right? . . . Well, well, . . ." answered Norina, openly bored and absentminded. She had no desire to advance into the labyrinth of history. What interested her much more were the looks and smiles that her husband and Leonia Macuto gave each other at the far end of the table. When a man looks at a woman he likes, every pore of his face smiles; smiles throng across it like an exultant crowd, it gives off warmth like the sun. Norina knew a thing or two; that mutual teasing was a prelude to something much more intimate. On her left was the Marquis Terzillo, who was thought to be an intellectual, since he had inherited a library from his uncle. He spoke with the slowness befitting those who know much, spacing his sentences so that the hearer felt as if he were having palpitations.

"A friend of mine, supposedly an intelligent and cultivated woman, which in fact she is—of quick intelligence and a vast culture almost unique for a woman—after having waited a long time before getting married, which everyone attributed to the fact that it was difficult for her to find a man worthy of herself, one that would stand up to her, finally decided to marry a moron, a man whose stupidity was renowned and becoming mythical. So from then on, people who had thought it a favor to have her company—she was desired by everyone—sighed reluctantly on sending her an invitation; because to the pleasure of her presence was joined the bother of having to stand her husband, who among other things talked a good deal and always beside the point, one gaffe after the other. Everybody thought the marriage couldn't last beyond a few weeks; but slowly they had to realize that it was a wonderful combination: perfect understanding and a very long period of mutual faithfulness. One fine day my friend finds herself a lover. At last! It was about time! Finally she woke up, she made up her mind, everyone cried, breathing more easily. How could she have stood a fellow like that for such a long time? The man she chose for a lover was simply an idiot. Next to him the husband became a genius, seemed brilliant and witty, erudite: he at least would talk, beside the point and putting his feet in his mouth, but he would say something. The second would not go beyond one of those chuckles that indicate an absolute lack of brains, he was a specimen of feeble-mindedness worthy of a psychiatric institute. They have combined into a mechanism of such perfection as to be a shining example to mankind. To make one like it all the Swiss watchmakers wouldn't be enough. A perfectly harmonious triangle."

"I would like to meet the *third* man in your friend's life," said Norina, weary and ironic.

"She will find him, you can be sure that she will. This time will be less easy, but she will find him. One never reaches the bottom in this subject and there is always a further station along the road."

"Ha, ha, ha!"

"If my mother-in-law puts me again between two phonies of this caliber I will say I have a headache and have dinner in my room."

"Ha, ha, ha!"

At the Sequis' table, the habitual escort of the eighty-year-old Duchess of Ascoli was Count Gelsomino di Lucera who, although over seventy, did not seem more than fourteen years old. A tired, plucked, squeezed-out teenager, his complexion almost white, his head like a pool ball, he agitated his small translucent hands nervously while talking. The Duchess of Ascoli had a little blonde wig that looked like a basket of bibb lettuce fallen over her skull. Her front was as if gouged out by a terrific blow, and what had disappeared from there reappeared behind; she wore dresses with plunging backlines to display her last physical gift: a hump. Both spoke with a rolled "r" gathered in France at an early age.

"Women had graceful little umbrellas and fans on which gentle things were painted or embroidered: landscapes with shallow running waters that made one feel refreshed, flowers, birds, butterflies moving around with enchanting grace, with fascinating coyness. From everything radiated a scent of femininity similar to that of garden flowers. Today they wear tortoise-shell glasses like old lawyers, they walk with feet spread out like coachmen, soles well planted on the ground. They show their legs even when it would be better to have them hidden."

"Bean-stalks."

"And bodies like bales of cotton, without either manners or grace. Carrying bags in their arms."

"They have all been promoted to servants."

"Bags that are getting bigger and heavier."

"And they push them all over you in a really obscene way; just like at the marketplace."

"In a short while they will be going around carrying baskets."

"Crates."

"Perhaps they will carry them on their heads."

"Like in the backwoods."

"Loves never seemed to end, they often lasted the whole life long."

"Now, after the second time they are bored to tears, they

can't stand each other; to cut things short they would gladly send the other out through the window. And once apart, they can't remember what happened between them."

"Men used to fight for a woman, they wouldn't wince at the prospect of gambling their handsome features on a saber. They would stand for years and years below one window."

"Not any more."

"And there were those who even killed themselves for a woman."

"You bet. The only reasons for suicide today are financial ones. They do it instead of going to jail."

"Everything has gotten nauseatingly vulgar."

"A weak vulgarity without any character."

"You can't go into a public place without feeling disgusted, repelled, to the point of wanting to leave immediately."

"If I were forced to eat in a restaurant or to board a bus, I would get a stroke on the spot."

"Believe me, my friend, there are only two places left where one can live with some decency: Lausanne and Monte Carlo."

"*Monte Carlo c'est Lausanne à la mer.*"

"*C'est ça,*" the Duchess went on, "if I couldn't spend some time in those two places every year I would feel lost."

"As long as the Communists won't come to spoil everything."

"One can meet there people with whom one can talk about a world that was so different. I can count on friends who can remember when France wasn't a republican democracy."

"When I think that on the streets I will get hundreds of blows from those damned shopping bags, I feel like locking myself at home."

Mrs. Sequi stretched her open hand on which she placed five kisses that she sent out to fly towards them: "My children," she used to call the Count and the Duchess, for whom she had a particular predilection.

"Ha, ha, ha!"

"The consommé was a true delicacy, it can't compare to anything I remember, and the sauce of this fish leaves one speechless, a flavor that the palate won't forget."

"So financiers, too, enjoy good cooking."

"Especially when it is of such quality as yours. I would like to know how this sauce was made."

"My cook doesn't keep any secrets, he will tell you very easily what to do. But if you or I were to try to make it, keeping exactly to the recipe, the sauce wouldn't be the same. That cook knows it and just laughs. I never argue with him, I like to treat him familiarly, we joke a lot . . . and one has to use a great deal of patience. He looks at me with a smirk on his face, it's the worst teasing I have ever had, I can't tell you what I feel moving inside, but I'll take it. Only from him, though. Cooks are like women who have caught a male: if you have an appetite you have to stand my tantrums, my dear. I have an urge to kick him where the sun won't shine, but when I sit down to eat a little sauce like this one I feel like smiling . . . and I don't mind."

Baroness Costanza also had a permanent escort at the table, the young Marquis Ali di Famagosta. For ten years she had been claiming to be betrothed to him, although she was sixty and he only twenty-eight. When the Baroness accepted an invitation she added a condition: Ali has to sit with me because if he happens to be next to someone he can't stand he will suffer, get ill, and I will have to nurse him for a week. Ali was burdened with an outstanding personality: he was acutely ultra-sensitive. Anything could upset him and as soon as he said, "This upsets me," he would begin to suffer right away. Any traffic with men was for him impossible, out of the question; that with women only irritated him.

Baroness Costanza wore a tight, short skirt, a dinner jacket

138

with white shirt and black tie, and she had an inch and a half of salt-and-pepper hair cut short at the nape of her neck. She never went to a hairdresser, but sat with great satisfaction in barbershops among men whom she intimidated. She was big, sturdy, with awesomely wide low-heeled shoes, a monocle and a whip with which she trained mastiffs at her villa.

Ali had the most golden blond hair one ever saw; when he reclined on a pillow a river of gold ran over it; otherwise it flew in the air disheveled. The skin of his cheek was a velvety light pink, his eyes were blue, large, beautiful. They mirrored the sky in all its depth. His gait was wavy, watchful and always uncertain, as if he feared some danger at every step. The Baroness was madly in love with him. As soon as he said, "This upsets me," he would coil up like a snail, and no matter where he was he had to be taken away. And the least cause was enough to upset him, the most unlikely: clashing shades of color, a draft, the handle of an umbrella or a doorknob, the presence of a disagreeable person—but then everyone was disagreeable because he hated the human race as a whole. He only loved the Baroness and Mrs. Sequi. Mrs. Sequi called him "my little blue angel," and had for him a fiery liking. On the Via Veneto the Baroness was known as "iron sergeant," and he as "mimosa." While with everyone else she had rude manners and harsh words, Costanza's every word to Ali was a soothing gush, a gentle croon; she became tender and soft to avoid hurting, in any way, his exceptional personality. "Dear love, my pet, precious, do you like it here? Do you feel at ease? Is this place agreeable with your taste? If not we'll leave. Tell me right away if there is anything wrong, don't worry about disturbing me, don't worry about anything."

Their love was born at the Lake of Albano while Ali was a guest in the villa of the Baroness. He hated the sea, he thought it brutal, tragic, violent, dirty, obscene; the waters of a lake

—provided it wasn't too large—were his favorite environment, nowhere else did he feel as much at ease. They spent most of the day on those quiet waters. The Baroness had Ali lie down in the bow of the boat over a mass of pillows: "Are you comfortable, Love? Do you feel soft, the way you like it? How is this breeze? Isn't it too strong? How handsome you are when you are like this. Do you want another pillow for your head?" Ali always answered, "Yes," he found everything beautiful and comfortable. Sunk into the pillows and lightly stirred by the cradle-like motion of the boat, there was nothing that could upset him. The Baroness, who in the country usually wore pants, after having settled him down took off her jacket, pulled up her sleeves, grabbed the oars, and began to row, letting her muscles dance. In such blessed peace, between the blue of the sky, the mirror of the water, and the green of the shore, Ali watched the Baroness with half-open eyes: "When are we getting married?" His voice was that of an angel: "When will you marry me, Costanza?" "Phooy," muttered the Baroness, "marriage is a serious thing. You have to be careful, my little one, you shouldn't rush such a delicate matter. One never thinks long enough about it. Don't get upset, Precious; be sure that when it's time for it we'll do that too. I never let you down, did I?" Looking over the rippling muscles of the Baroness, Ali smiled without getting upset.

"Ha, ha, ha!"

On Prince di Santo Stefano's right was Duchess Irene delle Fratte, a luxuriously provocative, mature beauty.

"Only you could solve a puzzle that keeps worrying me. For a great number of years I have been confessing the same sin, but the penance is always different."

In turning toward her the Prince had a shadow of a smile on his lips, the kind that children succeed in extracting from the least-smiling people.

"Don't you have your own confessor?"

"Excellency, I don't."

"Why so?"

"As I told you, my sin is always the same, it never changes; if I were to confess to the same priest I wouldn't have to open my mouth. We would become like a vending machine where one drops a coin and out comes the candy bar; therefore I go to a different confessor each time. The sins are identical, and I always get a different penance."

"It's all very simple and natural. The priest interprets your attitude, the state of your soul, from the way you announce your sin, from the very tone of your voice. So it happens that one decides a strict intervention to be necessary, while the other feels that leniency would be more effective in touching your heart. But are you sincerely regretful at the time you confess?"

"Well, I guess so . . . yes . . . like everybody else. I do regret it with my mouth, at the same time I know that I will give in again. I could tell precisely the time it will happen, while I'm confessing: today at five . . . tomorrow evening."

"This way you will end up in the Lord's disgrace."

"I am there already, and have been for a long time. But it's the Lord himself who creates the disgrace. I didn't make myself. I have always given in, I can't even remember the first time. All my life has been a succession of falls, I have been born to fall, it would seem the Lord made me for this purpose."

"No, no, we do possess certain tendencies but we have to fight them with all our powers until we dominate them, instead of being complacent and letting them drag us along. This is the Lord's way, the one that will save our souls. In the other direction lies the surest road to perdition."

"And with time it's only getting worse, Excellency; by now I give in like a burst door."

141

"Ha, ha, ha!"

Mrs. Sequi, who had overheard the last words of the Prince, wished to add something to the conversation.

"My friend, so far nobody has been able to change the way life works. Keep it well in mind that the instincts will always win out—just look around and see."

"And they will lead to perdition."

"I don't believe so little can ruin a soul."

"You forget that there are others."

"We don't know what the Lord will do, because he hasn't told anyone yet, but we know very well what he has done. Who are the others? They only want to make one pay a bitter price for one's victories, but it's all envy. Remember this: it's all envy."

"Ha, ha, ha!"

She raised a hand with uplifted finger:

"I am very religious!" Her declaration was so forthright as to attract the attention of half the table. "But I see a much more generous Lord than you do."

"A Lord catering to our every pleasure and whim, to all our comforts and weaknesses."

"Why not? I am sure he likes comforts too, and when he sees us good and cozy down where he placed us he enjoys it a little, he's the first to be glad about it. That's how it must be!"

"Ha, ha, ha!"

The Duchess delle Fratte had on her right Fiorelli, a painter who, after having achieved a mediocre artistic success, was improving on it with a splendid social career. A handsome boy, he knew how to dress with a pretended casualness that fell short of disturbing middle-class feelings. He was able to assume a tinge of snobbery, which made him look in the eyes of the bourgeoisie as a pleasant concession to the mistrusted

142

world of the intellect. He had made the portraits of all the members of the Sequi household, young and old. The hostess treated him as a friend and used to call him the painter of the royal family. Through her good graces many friends and acquaintances had asked him to paint their portraits. He could do them with an easy shrewdness that subtly fed the twin vanities of the soul and body, both equally absurd. She had been the first of his paying models, and had told him in clear terms: "I have a lot to do, I can't grant you more than four sittings, each one about one hour long. And ... let's get one thing straight: I won't see myself with my nose under a shoe."

"How is it that you painters get your inspiration?"

"Through the beauty of the object."

"I have seen paintings with only a bottle in them. What great beauty can there be in a bottle?"

"For a painter there is beauty in everything; he has to be able to see it and make others see it."

"And I have seen portraits of people who were ugly enough to scare you."

"The model was ugly but the painting beautiful, because the painter's art was beautiful. Raphael painted the Fornarina and other luscious girls of his age, but he achieved greater beauty by painting Pope Julius II, an old man with a goatee."

"But don't you feel better when you paint people you like?"

"Especially if they are women."

"Is that so?" laughed the Duchess, and Fiorelli leaned towards her to strengthen his case:

"You see, Duchess, a woman appeals simultaneously to the man and to the artist; and it's just when these two powers join that he dreams of a masterpiece. Think of when artist and model face each other alone in the studio, with the joint task of defying time by fusing together into an image of eternal beauty." He talked with growing warmth and from a decreas-

143

ing distance, while the Duchess began to issue forth spurts of laughter which were deeper each time, a gurgling that rose from deeper and deeper regions—the laughter that in women usually comes before a period of strenuous silence. At the end of his speech she turned to Mrs. Sequi.

"Pia, your painter is all right."

"I know, and I can see another portrait coming. I put him next to you on purpose. I am not an expert, but I love artists who think of life as an adventure, even if they risk breaking their necks in the process."

Noticing that the Prince was caught between two fires, the Duchess gave him a cue, trying to conceal the effort with which one approaches a dangerous animal:

"Don't you like painting, Excellency?"

"Yes, I do like real painting, as the geniuses of the past used to practice it. There are religious paintings of lasting greatness."

"But not only religious paintings are great."

"From the moment painting ceased to be religious it started to decay, so that now it has reached a childishness that borders on idiocy. People who admire it are even greater idiots than those who paint. Art loses all reason for being if it's not animated by a great feeling."

"Ha, ha, ha!"

The Duchess turned abruptly to Fiorelli:

"And what do you say? Don't you answer anything?"

"In such cases Christianity has taught me not to answer."

"Darling! What a dear! Pia, I really do like your painter."

"I know, I know."

"I hear, my dear lady, that your presence is very much desired in our office; they say that they haven't had the pleasure of seeing you for a long time."

"Do my contributions arrive regularly?"

"They do, but contributions aren't enough. Real charity needs direct participation to be effective."

"You really think that those poor devils care a lot about my being there?"

"Without a doubt."

"Well, I don't agree. Do you really believe that someone who is ill housed, ill fed, ill cared for when sick, is so happy to see ladies drive up to his den in some plush car, protected by soft furs in the winter?"

"Certainly. Contributions are indispensable on the material level, but participation is a moral act that is worth even more."

"Those who do charity with other people's money think so, anyway."

"If you were to send five to someone who owns nothing, his first thought will be: Why didn't I get ten? If you sent ten: Why not a hundred? On the other hand, if you are there to give with your hands, your help becomes a gesture of understanding, of sharing, of brotherhood. By being personally concerned with him, for the moment you share his circumstances."

"Yes, for the moment. I would like to know what he says when I turn my back."

"He would only express his gratitude, and whatever your gift was, it would seem large and welcome."

"One wouldn't think you were such an optimist."

"People who live comfortably believe that if poverty exists it's not visible. But only because they'd rather not see it, they prefer not to see it, they refuse to see it. You should come one morning with us and see the places where we bring help; you will see whether there is poverty or not."

"I told you before, Excellency, and I will keep telling you: I don't care for the show of misery. To me it isn't something to play around with, it isn't a hobby, but something to fight with all one's strength. One should be ashamed of poverty,

I am ashamed of it. I wish I had the strength to destroy it so I wouldn't have to hear about it any more; I would give everything I have so I wouldn't smell its stench. But if I were to give my last lira, there would only be one more poor devil and there would still be misery. I will die with this thorn in my flesh, with this wish"—she banged her hand on the table making the plates tremble and everyone turn towards her, "Dammit!"

"Ha, ha, ha!"

In order to quiet down she turned to her left-hand neighbor. Between her and the Prince a continuous latent battle went on; with the other there was the possibility of a friendly understanding.

"Is there still something you want from life?"

The famous financier settled his features in a youthful expression of shy inexperience before answering; he seemed to be fifty years younger when he answered, overcoming his embarrassment:

"I would like to be paid by a woman."

Mrs. Sequi drew back and stared at him speechless, as if she had just heard a most unlikely thing. The Prince was able to irritate her with his speeches, this one had succeeded in baffling her. She spoke with an effort, uncertainly:

"Well, I . . . when I was on the barricades I wanted to do what I pleased, I didn't use to care about the other's pleasure . . . it wasn't at all important to me."

The banker looked at her with increasing interest. And she, returning his stare, made the satisfied gesture of someone who has finally solved a problem. She spoke directly into his ear:

"You must have screwed a lot in your day."

"Ha, ha, ha, ha, ha!"

They all thought that she had bit him.

Understanding was established, and they laughed long together like the good fellows they were:

"Ha, ha, ha, ha, ha!" claiming again the attention of the whole table.

"Ha, ha, ha, ha, ha!"

The hostess alone was able to attain such a result.

"As soon as they start to play around, you come into my study with me. I want to show you some plans for stamping out poverty."

When everybody was about to raise his glass for a toast, Mrs. Sequi decided to appease the most illustrious of her guests, the Prince. He, whose evening meal usually consisted of coffee and cream, had sipped the delicious consommé like everybody else, but afterwards had only taken, out of courtesy, about two grams of every course, toying all the while with a breadstick. And he only drank water, so that his wineglass had been empty: Mrs. Sequi poured into it half of her champagne, then touched the rim of her glass to his in token of complete appeasement:

"Drink up, Excellency: good health and prosperity."

When the Prince and Checco had arrived at the bottom of the villa's staircase, a servant had led His Excellency to the upstairs apartments, while another took charge of Checco and led him in the opposite direction, as if he were taking care of the master's dog after a walk. It made the Prince feel sad and ill at ease. Not even the Pope separated him from his comrade in the solemn ceremonials of the church; it was frustrating to have to leave him for a social dinner.

Checco was taken to the servants' hall, next to the kitchen bustling with the operations of the great meal.

The help of the Sequis had finished eating an hour before; in serving the masters' dinner the odors did not make their mouth water, because the movements involved in offering and withdrawing dishes aided actively the digestion of their own meal, about which no one had ever complained in that house. Fine treatment, generous salary, tasks well divided and plenty of free time. Those who still nurtured gratitude in their hearts insisted that Mrs. Sequi was a mother for them rather than an employer. The few who had worked for her more than thirty years added that her heart was larger than her house. Whenever one of them had been sick and the doctor suggested the hospital, Mrs. Sequi had answered: "Hospital nothing. Is it an infectious disease? No, therefore he stays here with me, I will take care of him in my own home." And she took care of him in person, doing everything she would have done for one of the family. Many were the times that she had gotten out of bed at night to check on them, or to give a needed injection, at which she was better than a nurse.

Checco ate alone at the long table, a corner of which had been set for him. He was not given the servants' fare, but everything that the guests at the masters' table were served was brought to him, including a glass of champagne they kept for him at the bottom of a bottle. He laughed the whole evening long, trying to refuse the courses but tasting a little of everything: "I'm not used to it, I'll burst, it will make me sick." "Just taste this fish, it's sole, costs a thousand lire a pound. Get a taste of this gravy, it's better than cream, come on, just a little. Taste this rabbit pie. Checco, I saved half a quail for you, I saved you a pheasant breast, it's tender as butter, just feel it." He tasted a little of everything and kept saying: "Goody, goody," as he said to the children of Via Monserrato at Christmas and Easter, when he nibbled the crumbs of the masterpieces he had just finished dividing. The offer of wine he accepted more readily. The exquisite beverage warmed and strengthened him as it made his head spin cheerfully, and he gave in readily to the fellows' insistences. When the dinner was over and the guests had moved to the sitting rooms, the servants who were free began a game around him in the kitchen.

"Checco, it's true you're a virgin?"

"You never slept with a woman?"

"Would you like to sleep with this one?" They carried a laughing and resisting maid to him.

"Look, Checco. Mean anything?"

"Feel how hard it is." She tried to free herself and run away, while they showed Checco bounties that usually make men eager. But Checco took everything laughing like a child, in total innocence, without answering.

Until they came for him. His Excellency was the first one to leave. At a quarter to midnight Norina's cream-colored car was ready, waiting for him. He had to be in bed early, since at six in the morning he had to serve Mass. As he reached the bottom of the staircase he returned into himself and a great lightness enveloped him. A servant led Checco back to him, as one leads a dog to the master leaving for a walk. Only the leash was missing, but for all intents and purposes it could have been there.

ADULTERESS

NORINA WALKED in as she had never done before: hurried and absent-minded. She greeted Checco negligently and he watched her cross the hall with a tension in her steps which he had never seen before. The illiterate peasant noticed every shading in the behavior of the people he loved. They weren't the steps of the little miss looking forward to the sweetness of a carefree hour spent with her father, under those roofs where she was born and where now she used to feel so far away from everything, outside time and almost outside reality. As he could not keep up with those steps, she reached the door alone, and entered without being announced.

150

The Prince sat at his desk with a book open in front of him, meditating upon, rather than reading, the Letters of Saint Catherine of Siena. At the unexpected visit, instead of getting up to greet the caller as was his habit, he remained sitting and turned to Norina a questioning glance. And she didn't run to embrace him as had been her habit as a child, and as still was, but threw herself on the leather sofa which, instead of absorbing her voluptuously, reacted with a hostile hardness that made her bounce awkwardly: "You think you can make out with me? Forget it!"

"It's done."

The Prince arose slowly, not to sit by her but to stand up and face her inquiringly.

"What is done?"

"You know what."

"I don't know anything."

"Your memory is playing tricks, I explained it to you right here two weeks ago."

"What have you explained? What have you done?"

"I cuckolded my husband. A very simple thing."

The old man could not suppress a gesture which at any other time he would have thought unseemly on his part.

"Oh!" His hand went instinctively to his brow, to hide something he felt turning in there like a propeller. "Oh!" He seemed not to believe what she was saying.

"It isn't true, it can't be true, you didn't do that, it's impossible. . . . You just want to play a little joke on your father, a whim suggested to you by your old father and his old house." He almost smiled waiting for the answer.

"It's not a joke, I am in no mood for it; what I say and do is for real."

Her tone was so serious that the Prince let himself go on a chair, fearing to be felled by the sensation of emptiness

151

creeping over him. He kept smoothing his forehead to counter-act the increasing cold that was about to freeze his thoughts. His words seemed to be directed more to himself than to his daughter.

"Can it really be the truth? How could you have done something so grave . . . and tell me about it so lightly. What do I have to hear from the lips of my adored daughter, my little one. . . . You have been stricken by a bout of madness, you must be crazy, it can't be otherwise."

"I am anything but crazy. My action followed a rigorous plan, prepared and nurtured for a long time. Its conclusions were eagerly anticipated."

"These words I must hear through the lips of my little one. . . ."

For the first time he seemed to have lost the courage and rationality that were present in his every action. He was vague, dreamy.

"I must hear this from you. . . ."

"Don't you remember? Yet I told you that you would be the first one to know. I kept my promise."

"I would have gladly done without such privilege. Haven't you run to your confessor?"

"Not yet."

"But you are not yourself any more, I can't recognize my daughter."

"Don't think for a moment that this is the end, you have to know everything. This is only the beginning for your daughter, the party is just starting."

"Go, run to your confessor right away, tomorrow, better tonight, you haven't got a minute to lose, you are in God's disgrace."

"Don't worry, I'll go, but there is no hurry."

"Tell him that in a moment of aberration in which the Lord

had not sustained you, you had committed a sin unaware of its weight. Tell him that you are sincerely, deeply repentant, beg him to reconcile you with God, to Whom you must make the holy vow of never again falling into such infamy. May His help and pardon allow you to forget."

"I will go, don't worry about it. If you remember, I told you that you would be the first to know about it, that you are my confessor, Daddy."

"And what can I do? What can a poor man, a sinner, do? I can only pray God to enlighten you, to give you grace, and to forgive a woman who has lost her mind."

"I will go, on this issue you shouldn't worry. And if he will want to be reasonable, I'll be too; if not, I won't have a bone in my throat. I have plenty to tell him. My thoughts have been piling up in my head for fifteen years; I ask nothing better than to have the opportunity of airing them with someone who should know. My head is so full that it's ready to burst, and it will at the slightest chance."

The Prince had never been so lost and pained in his whole long life. He tried without success to find himself, shook his head looking distraughtly for something in the room . . . in the air. . . .

"My little darling . . . what have you done . . . you have spoiled everything."

"I couldn't have, there was nothing to spoil."

"You have spoiled everything by spoiling yourself."

"I feel exactly the same as I did before."

"The same as before? After having been on intimate terms with a man who wasn't your husband?"

"It was an experience like any other, an experience that I had to go through."

"Your words stem from a dark resentment which befogs your mind. If it were not so, they would indicate that your unclean

153

action has made you cynical, perverted, that it has made of you a lost woman."

"Daddy, one should not use too big words for the common events of everyday life. Otherwise we lose the proportion and perspective of things, and we are left without the elements for making a judgment. My husband is ready every day for such an unclean action, for such an infamy. Yet I wouldn't call him either cynical or perverted and even less lost: on the contrary he is a man who finds himself, it's a wonder how well he can find himself, and how often."

"I told you it's not the same thing."

"But it is. We are two people living next to each other and bound by the same pact; our aspirations, desires, and needs have the same value."

"What your husband has done is certainly to be blamed, but it doesn't have the same value, the same consequences or the same responsibility. Your sin is unforgivable; besides having soiled yourself forever you could bring an illegitimate son into your family."

"So my husband will keep this illegitimate son, since it was he who taught me how to get one. Poor Daddy, you really don't know anything about life, I told you so often you weren't up to date. As soon as my husband will know he will think that I did the right thing, and probably he is wondering why I didn't do it before. He will feel that our relationship is finally cleared up, become perfect. He will be relieved to know that he doesn't owe anything to me any more."

"You're talking nonsense. See what effects your act has had on you. A young woman who is forgotten, abandoned, despised by her husband and without strong education and virtue, could easily fall into the despicable error of looking to other men for the affection and tenderness that she could not find and misses. We could be lenient with such a woman, but not in your case:

154

you said yourself that your husband has affection and respect for you, he doesn't despise or forget you. . . ."

"There is something for me too, when he remembers, among all the women in the world I am there, too, and probably I am not the one he likes least—at one time anyway he did like me. Once in a while my turn comes, and he doesn't do it because of duty or to humor me, you know, or because I entice him in any way. I don't know how, but he remembers me once in a while, I am one of the features on the program. As you see, I don't feel like a wife to him any more: it's more like being a union member, like belonging to a cooperative. Well, that's not enough for me, can't you understand? It's not enough."

"Will you see that man again?"

"Perhaps I will . . .perhaps I won't. Maybe. He hopes I will, anyway."

"Is he married? Does he have a family too?"

"No, he's a bachelor, he is seven years younger than I. You should see, Daddy, what a man, proportioned like a Greek statue."

Now and again the Prince shut his eyes tight, wishing for them to stay forever closed.

"I can still choose, and I did choose well, you can be sure I didn't make a mistake. Of all the men within my range I chose the most handsome; he's extraordinary, exceptional."

"You see how your sin is twice as bad as his, three times as bad. . . . There is no measure to evaluate it."

"I told you it's just the start, dear Daddy. Next I will have a married man, and then the infamy will be twice or three times as great, whichever you wish, but it will be the same on both sides: equal."

"Never, never, that you can be sure of. Your fault will always be infinitely more grave than the man's, no matter who the man is, and you will find that out by yourself, it won't

155

take you long. The later it happens the worse it will be for you."

"I will go through four, five, six men . . . ten, a dozen . . . or I will go on with the same one, who knows. . . . Until the day comes to give up and balance the accounts."

"Where did that man take you? Where did you let yourself be led? I hope you haven't soiled the holiness of the conjugal roof?"

"No roofs, Daddy, no soiling, the sanctuary is safe. And he did not take me anywhere, I went there myself under my own power. It was in his house, a delightful bachelor flat: it was perfect, it had everything that a woman might wish or need under the circumstances. It wasn't like this place, this desert, where I can't find a piece of mirror to fix my hair after you have mussed it up."

"Yes. You climbed those stairs that a little earlier, or a little later, a prostitute had climbed or will climb. You have descended to her level."

"For the time being I'm not a prostitute, and I don't think I could ever become one. But I am a woman who has been faithful to her husband for fifteen years, and who wants a little fun, a little freedom before becoming old, before being left in a corner unwanted. My partner is not for prostitutes, anyway he doesn't need them with his body, his twenty-seven years and his position. He's adventurous, he can be selective, at least I think so. But I wouldn't bet on it; men take anything as long as it's a change, and probably he too likes to go from one to the other."

"To find himself in the end with the usual handful of flies."

"The handful of flies that we all find ourselves with in the end."

"It's not true!"

"The only bright point of my adventure has been that I found out at thirty-five that I am a very, very lively woman," she

156

raised her voice for her own benefit, "and now I understand why my husband hasn't forgotten me completely, why sometimes I matter to him. And this isn't your handful of flies, Daddy. One takes what life offers, if one doesn't take the chances in time life won't give anything. I'm still a woman with a long way to go. As for the rest. . . ." Young Mrs. Sequi bowed her head and shook it in deep hopelessness, "as for the rest . . . my experiment has not worked out. Unfortunately, I still like my husband. Worse, I like him even more. This is the knot of the problem. My whole experience seemed to have only one effect: to set up a comparison which was flattering to my husband. This is really bad, I am almost afraid to tell you, but it's true. I couldn't let go, part of myself was always tense, as if I was looking for elements of comparison that would allow me to reach an ultimate decision. And I can't blame my choice, I couldn't have chosen better; the fear of such a result had made me very difficult, very discriminating. I had an instinctive fear that things would turn out this way; perhaps I went to him with disillusion in my pocket. After this I hoped to feel detached, far from my husband. Instead I feel closer, caught; I realized that there isn't anything about him I don't like, I want him more than ever."

It seemed that the Prince was unable to speak or think, and least of all to listen to his daughter. His eyes were kept closed tightly so as not to see the void opening everywhere around him. His daughter and her voice appeared strangely distant and distorted in the fog. After the last words he seemed to wake up, fired by a strength welling from his soul.

"But of course, sure, after your unspeakable aberration you like your husband even more because it's him you love, it's him you have loved first, it was him you had chosen in your purity. Because you did such a wrong to him you love him more; if you were to roam the world you couldn't find a man

157

who could make you forget him. You can't love anyone else and yet you have hurt him, you have raised a permanent shadow between the two of you. Against your own self you have cleaved a rift in your sacred union."

"Please note that if I made a rift, he has built a hill of broken pieces."

"And I will keep on repeating that a man's actions do not have the same value as a woman's."

"And I will keep on repeating that after a certain point a woman will do what she can: she'll make do. Your law made by and for men is too comfortable."

"What did you get from this making do? What good has your folly been to you? You still like your husband best, just as for him you are the only woman. Even if he has to grovel with a hundred more women first, eventually he will know that you had always been his woman. The others he will forget, or remember with a commiserating smile, a sad smile for them and for his own weakness. And he will still be yours, forever, you will be eternally each others' whatever you do. And you say you haven't spoiled anything: you have spoiled your love, and in this life you couldn't have spoiled anything more beautiful. You thought who knows what marvelous views would open, and you found a wall barring your sight. It's your punishment, you were punished and now you can only retrace your steps."

"This is only what happened to me on the first time. I told you it was only the beginning for your daughter...." Norina played with the words as if they were candies in her mouth. "I can't leave it at that."

"If your husband fails and lets himself go you have to increase your love for him and your virtue. You have to be more virtuous, do his share too, love him for his mistakes and his sins. Here is your greatness: you will think with pride that the Lord gave you an opportunity to prove it. You will feel a strength that nothing can abate, that nothing can win or diminish. You will witness the miracle of his return, repentant and disillusioned, his heart full of admiration and esteem. How could you influence him after you had failed yourself? It will end in mutual contempt and accusations, any possibility of love will be lost. The Devil must have shown you the wrong path, and you have been duped. You are in his hands, you'll have to get out of them."

"I have taken the right path, the true and only one. Sometimes the Devil can give good advice, too."

"It won't take you long to realize its quality."

"So I should sit back and take the leftovers of all the other women who enjoy my husband under my nose, knowing that when he won't be able any more, as a stupefied wobbly old man he will come back to me to have his gout or his asthma taken care of. No, no, a hundred times no. But I have to tell you something else: my liking for him is somehow related to those fatheads around him who give him the eye. Although I feel like setting fire to their skirts, they lend him a fascination which appeals very much to me. You see what a contradiction, our hidden emotions are always fighting against each other, we carry the war within ourselves. If my husband were a serious, quiet man working at his desk all day long, or reading works of science or religion—can you imagine what a bore it would be? I wouldn't like him as I do now. I appreciate and admire the fine qualities of a man who is controlled by his mind or his conscience; but I wouldn't want to go to bed with him. I would feel something cold next to me, and I need warmth, very much warmth. I know it's a contradiction, but deep down I like the wrongs my husband is doing me."

"If you like them, keep them because you deserve it. You

speak of your husband as if he were an animal, a horse or a dog, or something."

"Not exactly horse or dog, but the animal has a share in this game, and how. It's a question of senses, dear Daddy: of skin, touch, sight—and you keep talking about clouds. To a woman the spiritual values you talk about are very vague and questionable, hard to understand and often harmful; they produce misunderstandings and can decay into a stinking mess. There is a midpoint between animal and man made of pure spirit, where perhaps we can get together. My husband's carefree amorality has a certain appeal."

"You forget that these amoral, sensual, selfish men who let themselves be led by the material values in life want all the freedom for themselves. Woe to the wife whom they discover cheating on her promise. They become mean and ready for any violence."

"No, no, don't worry, you won't see your daughter's name in the crime reports; there is no danger of violence. I told you, you aren't up to date, you are at least a century behind. If things were as you think, I would have betrayed him long ago, or at least would have pretended to; I can still be a flirt if needed, but in my case it won't help. Instead, my unhealthy action will bring ease, peace, and balance to our lives. When my husband will notice it, he will ask himself why did it take me so long to take this resolution."

"Didn't the image of your children appear as you were climbing those stairs?"

"I didn't even think of it, Daddy; I was thinking of something else."

"Haven't you seen your daughter's face barring your way?"

"There weren't any faces, the road was clear."

"Just think if your little girl were to know what her mother has done."

160

"My little girl, whom I love very much, is herself a woman like her mother, and she will face her fate as a woman. She will pursue the same career."

"A fine example you are setting to your child. You couldn't reproach her if someday she were to fall, you could only strike your breast and say: *mea culpa*."

"That's not true either, or at least not completely. Setting an example counts up to a point, but what counts more is the way events take place."

"Aren't we the makers of these events? We are the events. Hour by hour we build or demolish our happiness. It depends on us, not on vague outside forces to which we can only bow in resignation. Responsibility for what we do is ours only."

"You will admit in my case it's only half."

"It is only and completely yours. If the wife is good, every man who has acted wrongly will eventually return to her, and become aware of her beauty and greatness. A revelation then occurs, starting a new cycle; that of love cleansed and purified of needless matter, lived entirely in the spirit: the most beautiful love."

"Of course, they will return to their wives after they have lived on the fat of the land and are too tired to do anything; as disjointed and soft old men they will return to have their ills cared for. The wife waits on the sidelines looking on, because towards the end of the game she will be allowed to work with all her virtue on the field of his loves carrying hot tea, ointments and wet packs, enema on the ready, and enjoy the most beautiful stage of life, the one made of pure spirit. I'm afraid they don't make women like that any more; if you find one be sure to hold her tight and don't let her go without giving her a well-deserved diploma for idiocy. You act as a counsel for men, for the same reason I defend women. But my problem is different, much more serious, and unrelated to our digres-

161

sions. After what I've done I still like my husband. This is too much, it really worries me: the passage of time and events, rather than fading his appeal, only makes it stronger."

"Then you admit that your thoughtless act has left only disgust and bitterness in your soul."

"No, no, easy on the disgust, there was no disgust involved. I am not silly, I told you that I chose well, I couldn't have chosen better. However, I must say that it didn't come out as I planned, since I never liked my husband better."

Suddenly the Prince sprung to his feet and hurried to sit with his daughter on the cranky sofa. He embraced her, pulling her head close to his own.

"My little darling . . . my little one . . . . You are like your mother, like your father, you wish your man all for yourself, and you are right, it should be that way. It's inconceivable how men cannot understand and appreciate such a fine and beautiful thing. You are just like your mother," he held and caressed her. "Do you know that if someone told her about a woman who had made the same ugly mistake as you have, out of spite, she wouldn't believe it, she could not believe it, it was beyond her imagination? And if she was shown the evidence she still refused to talk about it, she wouldn't even let the name of that woman be said in her presence. That is an instant of exalted abandon, which feels as if happening above us, beyond our will; it is an ecstasy from which life wells. It should only happen between two who have sworn everlasting love and faith to each other, whose bodies are one. If your mother had heard what you have told me she would have been broken by it, I am sure it would have made her ill; or perhaps she wouldn't have understood you, she wouldn't have believed you, she would have thought that you were only insane. No qualm had ever cast a shadow over our union based on certitude, to mistrust each other was a possibility alien to

162

us. How could you have forgotten it? To know that the other's life is for you, that he will never do anything that could harm or displease you, that every action, every thought of the day will be devoted to you, and that you can count on him in any event: that is what gives support, courage, strength to face life. When the union is true, misfortune, adversity, sacrifices, everything can be easily solved and settled."

While her father went on caressing her, Norina spoke dreamily.

"You see, Daddy, things didn't work out so well for you either. You and Mother were so much in love, you lived for each other, your union was true, yet death did part you."

"Parting was the last test: our love has become sublime through death. After your mother's death I haven't soiled my love even for a second with the thought of another woman. My little one, if I had such a thought even for a second I would reproach myself for it as for the basest thing, since it would have ruined the most beautiful; I would feel soiled even if I had lived through this second in the unconsciousness of sleep. The beauty of our love has remained pure and grows, it fills me with light every minute, every hour, every day. Your mother is also made of light, of light only, everlasting light; she has been looking over me from the time of our parting, she has always seen me and she waits for me with open arms, arms made of light. . . ."

Norina disengaged her head from her father's clasp to ask in a childlike voice:

"Tell me something, when you married Mother were you virgin as she was?"

For a moment the father bowed his head, then lifted it with confidence, and answered in such quiet and candid tones as if he were facing God rather than his own daughter.

"No. You see, Norina, in my times there used to be women

of quite amiable and reserved disposition who prostituted themselves to young men of good families answering the call of manhood. Some who were more rich and vain took these women from the shadows to show them off, exposing them to the world as exhibits of their own childish ambitions, competing with each other as to who could cover them more with jewels and feathers. The more serious youths' women were kept in the shadow, contented with a modest and withdrawn life, glad to make a nest egg with which they would buy an apartment to rent once their youth had faded."

"See, you weren't so pure either."

"But from the day I met your mother I never went back to those women. I had only one thought: to make myself worthy of her love and purity. To linger in thought on the memory of those women would have seemed filthy. But I had seen very young the true values of life; I wasn't so foolish as to exchange gold for tinsel."

Norina drew a long sigh:

"Yet, if you don't have true gold you have to get along with imitation, what can you do?" She passed her hand through her hair, "Now you have ruined my hairdo and there is no way for me to fix it. You should see the place I went the other day. There was everything, better than home. Someone who takes all that care must love women. You didn't love women, admit it, deep down you really didn't like them."

"I have loved one woman only, the one who was mine. But not for an hour—I loved her as I do now, forever."

After combing her hair Norina stood up and greeted her silent father, who seemed to be wanting to give final advice with his eyes.

She crossed the throne room with Checco. This time she walked very slowly, almost shuffling her feet. Instead of taking his arm, she placed hers over his shoulder.

"Good thing you stayed single. You were wise not to take a wife."

Checco laughed.

"Wise . . . why?" he thought. He was happy to feel that contact with the beloved little miss's hand.

"One can be wise in different ways," he said later. "If it hadn't been for your father, I would've been in a monastery for years." He talked with the pleasure of someone looking at a wonderful building that shines in sunlight far out in the country.

EST!

EST!

EST!

ABOUT TWO centuries ago
Abbot Fea, then in charge of the conservation of Roman antiq-
uities, decreed that a few hovels which were leaning against
the right wing of the Pantheon be torn down. (This should
not set a precedent to Overseers of Antiquity: hovels are the
best friends of monuments.) It seems, however, that Abbot Fea
had been justified in this particular instance, since the houses
were ready to fall on their own accord. As a result of his
order, at the foot of the hyperbolic range of columns and
around the side of the huge round building there was left for
several years a plot of earth waiting to be paved which, as
still happens, was never paved. Now this plot lent itself mar-

velously to certain needs that the people of the neighborhood went to discharge there—either because they loved fresh air, or their houses lacked conveniences; or just because passing by, they felt a sudden imperious call.

Finally the plot was paved and enlarged and given the name —which it still bears—of Via della Rotonda; but for years upon years every Roman, great or small, called it "Fea's shit-house." Even after the Abbot had departed from this world. Let's pass over the fact that a "shit-house" ought to be an enclosed place; we are not here to raise pedantic questions of purity in the field of philology, God help us: as long as words are being said they are the right words, they are wrong only when nobody uses them any longer. The reason for resurrecting this rather paltry anecdote is that it fits very well our purpose, to describe Rome and its people more clearly. Those who relieved themselves at the sides of the famous monument bearing the remains of, among others, Agrippa and Raphael, did not mean to lack respect nor to offend anyone. On the contrary, as we have already said, if we want to understand what is true, great and beautiful about these people we have to bear in mind as a central fact the reality of the human body, the sympathy with the materials out of which it's made; a love which is total acceptance, through which nothing is rejected or spoiled. And when for such a long time the street kept being called "Fea's shit-house," it was the right name, deserved, and no one implied with that name anything malicious or offensive either to the Abbot Fea, to the Pantheon, or to those who went to defecate there. It should be an honor and pride to this city that it never allowed Puritanical hate and ridicule to infect its spirit, nor will in the future, I hope. So if you walk into an inn, you are left speechless by the toast you hear from a middle-aged, happy, fat gentleman standing at a large table: "A dish of *rigatoni a la matriciana,* a quart of wine, and a good piece."

The first to cheer at the humming long table is his wife, smiling in candid agreement; she means to be noticed as a necessary component of her husband's toast. The foreigner would be surprised and dubious about the feasibility of the announced exercise, due to the fearsome size of the husband, and the even more awesome size of the wife. Probably these activities are released to public scrutiny when their execution has become problematic, or, rather, impossible.

If you want to know something about these people and enjoy them somewhat, before buying the map of the city you should buy the sonnets of Gioacchino Belli, the true guide of Rome. It's easy reading, educational and fun. Dante should be read to understand Florence and the Florentines; Belli, to understand Rome and the Romans. The first one never makes you laugh, the second makes you laugh all the time. And then get to know the inns.

Rome has no cafés, except the few that cater to the transients and to the small cosmopolitan crowd of Via Veneto. But be careful, because many of the inns, especially those whose address is known to everybody, are inns only in name and in appearance but their ambition is to increase their revenues by slowly changing into restaurants. At first they isolate, then they eject the people who are the soul of the inn, in order to substitute them with those who are the same around the world and bore everybody but themselves. One would make a big mistake believing to know Rome for having hung about such places; he would have missed the whole point and carried with him a distorted memory of Rome, unaware of what Roman blood means.

There is an outrageous number of inns, but the ones we mean can be most easily found between the Sistine and Palatine bridges, around the pine-shaded monument to the poet of this people.

Giggino, Giggetto, Guerrino, Romoletto, Carlone er pacioc-cone, Santino, Angelino, Pippetto . . . saying the innkeeper's name, the Roman citizen embraces him, and when the name is "lousy *Ghetanaccio*," he even gives him a kiss.

Sora Teta, sora Tota, sor'Elvina, sor Cecilia, sora Nanna, sora Nannetta . . . are the names of the saucy hostesses of Rome.

The inns mainly sell wine: especially *Est! Est! Est!* As long as there will be sun and wine the Roman won't be acquainted with sorrow. Every place you will find spaghetti and fettucine ready, or about to be ready; all of them have a cut of beef in the icebox for a cutlet or a steak; on the counter there is prosciutto and salami under glass. But the real inn sells wine above everything else, and it's the rule for the customers to bring the rest.

While the company settles down around the long tables exchanging loud greetings and hot news, the younger members are just arriving from home with huge bowls of pasta and spectacular salad bowls which when placed on the table take on the liveliness and pride of flags. And trays of pizza. The innkeeper begins his task, bringing glasses, pitchers, and bottles. The bottles of golden liquor of the Castelli make a noble crown around the food. It's a living room for those who lack one of their own but like to be together, the innkeeper's living room where people can meet and eat cheerfully in company.

The physical geniality is the first thing that one notices about them, a geniality that manifests itself in roundness everywhere. The men in general are quite round, but mature women, and the elder ones, are often of unbelievable proportions. Sitting on an ordinary chair, invisible under masses of flesh, instead of being a restful position, becomes a feat of balance and courage worthy of admiration. Although bloated with age, on their features are reflections of youthful beauty. As soon as they can, the boys lean on their elbows with proprietary airs, and the children whose chins barely reach the table top look like heads of Saint John brought to Herod's table by Salome.

Each head of family serves the little ones first, then his wife and finally himself; hardly does he start eating that a boy sitting next to him, who has already devoured his share, begins to fish with a fork in his father's plate. The father lets it happen a few times, he likes this fellowship with his son, and even more he likes to see him alert, greedy, and brave. But as the boy keeps the game up, finally he sets down a limit: "Didn't you eat yet?" The boy doesn't answer but nods "Yes" with his head and swallows in resignation. "So now just let me eat too." Great plates of spaghetti that look steeped in blood, salads on which the finest colors of the rainbow shimmer, golden pizzas.

The meal over, they keep on drinking. Invitations and offers are exchanged: quarts arrive from every direction, golden flashes that soon disappear. Conversations rise in volume and become meaty, their thoroughness borders on obsession as the action of the wine increases in the speakers. Women drink only few sips here and there just to stay cheerful, and they are happy; their husbands' well-being makes them feel good too. They look at the husbands with maternal expressions, like wet nurses whose highest happiness is to see the children well and amused.

The older boys and girls—tied by invisible yarns whose pattern can be easily discerned—the same who at the beginning had brought the bowls of pasta and salad, now come back again with guitars and accordions. There is no dancing in the Roman inn, but after dinner there is music and singing, and above all there is conversation and argument. The women have to talk louder and louder to be heard above the din that also increases, until the place is a bedlam of shouts, voices and song, music and laughter, all contributing to a happy sleep.

A need of opening themselves up comes over the men, the wine prompts them to confide all, tell everything to their friends, and as confidences grow heavier they repeat insistently: "You are my friend." You are my friend, therefore I can speak to you, I can tell you things that in your hands could become weapons against me. These reserved people, so careful in what they say or do, at the inn become expansive, they make you feel that friendship isn't dead, that it is an important value and a means of survival and resistance. "I don't give a damn about all the cops in Rome." "Who doesn't drink wine is blasphemous, because wine was consecrated by the Lord." They keep holding the glasses high. "I'll work when I feel like it." "When I'm in the mood my wife starts to give me a certain smile. . . . You girls have got something there . . . something there. . . ." And a need for being generous, for sharing everything with the friend in exchange for the binding emotion: "If you come tomorrow, I'll give you ten fish, what's ten fish? Perhaps two pounds of stuff. So I'm broke, but you can have it all. . . ." The conversations elope on tangents, here and there the history of the place emerges in the guise of allusions, quotes, anecdotes, examples; the history which the Roman seems to try shaking off like a dog shakes off water, unconsciously. It makes him maudlin, it gives him a touch of melancholy on the verge of happiness.

Guerrino, Giggino, Giggetto, Santino, Angelino, Romoletto, Carlone er procioccone stand in the center of the place, walk up and down with serious faces, then stop to get an over-all view with an authoritative glance. As they carry fresh quarts to the tables, their words and manners are curt. Everyone is ready to take quietly comments, reproaches, and often insults: one can discuss everything at the inn, but the innkeeper's authority is never questioned.

Two ten-year-old boys have retired to play cards at one table.

171

They hold and throw the cards like men, they look at each other with the intensity of one who wants to dominate without being in turn dominated. The innkeeper stops to warn them: "Watch out, fellows, in the other deck there is a missing card already." The boys wiggle their noses, shake their shoulders without answering, they throw the cards with an even more masculine movement.

THE
DUCHESS
OF ROVI

CHECCO HAD never appeared
before his master at once so puzzled and cheerful. He wasn't
able to talk; so he mumbled, shaking his shoulders:

"There's a lady ... a lady ... she says she's the Duchess
of Rovi. . . ."

The eyes and forehead of the Prince contracted violently,
while a foreign but very clear voice came through the open
door, saying teasingly:

"I came to see the ogre in his lair."

The Prince gathered his strength suddenly, and ran. Magda
saw him rushing towards her with such force, that, unable to
seize the situation, she began to back away, then turned around

173

to flee, but not fast enough for the Prince's foot to miss its target below the back.

As a result of the brief contact Magda went down the staircase giving a graceful display of her most airy dance steps. At the bottom she turned around. The Prince stared at her from above as one stares at a cat which has been kicked out for stealing. She bowed at him, laughing loudly.

"Adieu, mon petit chou, je suis quand même la Duchesse de Rovi et bientôt la Princesse de Santo Stefano."

In the background, Checco kept repeating to himself:

"She's a good one, she's a good one. . . ."

1 9 5 0

WHAT WAS happening
lately at the Santo Stefano Palace, where years and centuries
had gone by without leaving a trace? The people were still
the same, but something new showed through their features.
The lodgers kept going in and out, and Bice's friends gathered
to talk about Church events or to recite the rosary. They were
always the same but they came at different hours, their eyes
brimming with mystery. The old women's legs followed a
rhythm by which one would have thought that youth had
reawakened in their bones. Bice was nowhere to be seen.

In the first days of December an extraordinary object, which
kept everybody in a state of adoring confusion, arrived in the

175

porter's lodge. The Prince had appointed Bice to get his uniform ready for the forthcoming Opening of the Door. The Holy Year was to be ushered in, and in the lodge of Via Monserrato the preparations for it had begun. His Excellency's uniform was kept with religious care in a closet, or spread on the table for everyone to admire.

The first thing Bice did was to run to a convent of Sisters who were renowned for their needlework. The Mother Superior offered to do the job herself, but she read on Bice's face that the offer had filled her with grief. The Prince had bestowed such a trust on her, such an honor—she couldn't let anyone else take it away from her. If she had, it would have meant she was unworthy, would have shown that she couldn't do the job; it would have made her feel offended, displaced, reduced to a useless, despicable object. She only came to ask help and advice, nothing else; she wanted to be a match to the task. She returned with all sorts of little jars, special irons, balls of silk thread, black velvet patches, golden frogs and galloons.

The women formed a knot around the costume, and the lodgers kept visiting assiduously. Their faces all looked joyous and surprised, as if they were standing by the cradle of a baby.

The two weeks of work were peppered by endless discussions. They washed with alcohol the white feather of the hat, which had become gray over the years, and they curled it into shape over the fire. The long black silk hose were reviewed too, and found unraveled at the ankles: the repair was made with fastidious precision. And His Excellency's shoes, the ones with the silver buckles, were shined until they could reflect images. It was the ironing of puffs that faced the women with the worst problems, with crises of bewilderment and hopelessness. Hundreds of puffs made up the ballooning shorts, the sleeves and doublet, and the collar which looked like a hornets' nest and had to be ironed with starch. Bice had to run back to the convent a few more times, and at each return resumed her task with fresh heroism. At last it came to the polishing of the sword with its handle of gold, covered with jewels. They all wanted to hold it in hand several times, eyes closed as if they expected to get a shock from its touch, but what each felt were moments of enchanted ecstasy.

On the morning of the 23rd, towards noon, Bice climbed the staircase, carrying solemnly on her outstretched arms the restored uniform, wrapped in white cloth. Two hours before dawn the next morning, December 24th, people were swarming around the gates, and inside the porter's room women dressed all in black were chirping as in a birdcage. When the car with the Vatican plates arrived and the Prince appeared they drew up in two lines and stood in religious silence, not without admiring through lowered lashes the results of their feverish work. The ancient costume of the Santo Stefanos sparkled in renewed splendor, and the Prince, walking steadily and very straight, had a cheerful face that sheltered shadows of pleasant, far-away memories. Good old Orazio, otherwise known as the "Barber of Seville," had come in the darkness of early morning to shave him and set his hair with consummate art. His Excellency had asked him to take Bice's place and guard the palace during the ceremony, which was scheduled to last five hours. All the lodgers were going to St. Peter's, where each had his own place. As soon as the car started on its way, proceeding very slowly at a solemn pace, the group of women covered with black veils began to walk too, hands joined across their breasts, praying under their breath. Checco was the only one not to show anything new or different. As he got in the car behind his master, he was the same as he was every morning going to Mass or to the market, lacking only the folded satchel under his arm. He would stand for hours close to the throne, next to that spectacular man dressed in the costume of an ancient Roman patrician; he would walk like a great dignitary, with unmatched ease and the usual smile, behind the Pontiff carried in his chair under a canopy, in his richest robes, for the greatest solemnity of the Christian world. And if the Pope had happened to turn his eyes on Checco, he would have thought very natural his presence there.

The great ceremonies in St. Peter's are endless, yet they go by in a twinkling. After four, five, six hours, the spectators ask: "It's all over? Is there nothing else? They did it fast this time." Some people who feel something stir in the direction of their stomach answer: "But it's noon, we've been here since seven o'clock." Even those who have to stand lose all sense of time and of themselves.

It's a golden vision which takes you within itself; all light and song. The little woman who just came up from the country is saying the truth when she exclaims, "Thank you, Lord, I am in Heaven"; the cry comes from her heart.

The rite of the Holy Door, in all its complexity and inexhaustible wealth of detail, is surely the most impressive. Many hours pass from the arrival of the Pope to the moment when, chanting the first bars of the *"Te Deum,"* he climbs the chair on which he will be carried across the whole church with an almost unnoticeable movement to the altar of Saint Petronilla, from where he gives the Most High Blessing to all Christianity.

On leaving the Church one has the feeling of returning to the earth in rags, of shouldering again at the doors the burdens of life after a flying journey in a blessed, unbelievable land.

The Holy Year of 1950 had specific and exceptional meanings, coming as it did after such grave events and in the midst of one of history's most dramatic centuries.

The Pontiff presided over sixty-seven public ceremonies, but the one with the greatest significance occurred towards the end

178

of the year, on the morning of All Saints' Day: the "Ascension of the Virgin."

Such a crowd was anticipated for that day—and the previsions proved to be underestimated—that Saint Peter's was not thought to be large enough for it, and it was decided to hold the function in the square.

Those who know papal Rome also know that there is quite a difference between the ceremonies held in church and those held on the square. No matter how many religious implications St. Peter's Square has, and it does have many, it's still a square. People who love shows are more easily attracted to it, and they don't feel bound by the need for silence and respect that a religious function requires. On the other hand, the square allows outbursts of enthusiasm which could not be permitted in the church, and which, even if permitted, would be there out of place. Square and church are very different. The spectators feel that they aren't on consecrated ground, so they fill the endless periods of waiting with chatter and with remarks on all kinds of topics which in a church could not be mentioned. The square is ideal for greeting the Pontiff on Easter morning, for hearing an informative speech on morality—those who are acquainted with the lights of Rome know what the square can be at vespers or at high noon. But it distracts the attention in a religious ceremony, and changes its character. As one wipes one's feet on entering a hallowed place, so one has to wipe one's soul clear of criticism on entering St. Peter's. Still, one couldn't have chosen a more beautiful, more appropriate place than the yard of St. Peter's to proclaim the new Dogma, under the sky, directly into the light of the sun.

Once you are in the square, during the waiting which increases expectations to impatience, to exasperation, and eventually makes the event itself infinitely more satisfying, you have to be prepared to answer the most strange and unexpected

179

questions—some pointed, some naive—that people congregated from far and wide will ask. Most questions deal with the Pope himself, a being surrounded by a fascination that affects everyone; or with the fabled place in which he lives, that jumble of buildings massed one over the other, yet producing an effect of astonishing harmony. No architect could possibly create a building which would stimulate the curiosity and the imagination as much as that conglomeration of elements without any architectural affinity.

Where does the Pope live? Where does he sleep, eat, read, write, receive visitors? Which is the window of his room? Does he ever look out, and can he be seen if he does? The window is so high up that even when he does look out it's difficult for someone to see him, except for the Romans, especially those who live in the neighborhood. When the Pope returns to his quarters after a ceremony, he sometimes comes to his window to greet for the last time the crowd that on leaving the Basilica stops in the square to cheer him untiringly. Which goes to show that the long hours of waiting plus those of the ceremony had not been enough. You have to point out his window. Those of his room and of his library where the Pope works and which stays lit until the small hours of the night. Everyone knows that Pius XII eats little, sleeps less, and works a lot. Some people wonder at the sight of all those lightning rods on the roof. No other building has as many lightning rods as the Vatican. The presence of lightning rods is puzzling, and many a learned debate is heard on the subject. Some consider them a sign of skepticism, others think them completely useless. Someone adds that lightning rods are necessary for places where so many art objects of unlimited value are kept. Others claim that the rods do not pertain to the Pontiff, and that among the thousands who live in the immense palaces some sinner might well be hiding. The claim is answered by the contention that the Lord would never strike the Saint in order to punish a sinner. "That's right! You are well informed." There is one thesis fought with great ardor: "The Lord punishes the just so that the sinners will repent, He's always done it." But this thesis is not readily accepted, people shake their heads unsatisfied. "Didn't He sacrifice even His divine son for man's salvation? That's how the Lord works." Not even such a decisive argument commands agreement. Finally a large, fat man, health overflowing his face, intervenes in a voice that covers all others: "You can't ever be careful enough; storms don't give a damn who you are." The debate is closed.

The guards have begun to march out the Bronze Gate. They move in slow rhythm, and slowly weave a vast arc of color among the crowd. A group of French misses is all in titters, asking continuously: *"Qui sont ces messieurs?"* There are three corps guarding the Pontiff: the Palatine Guards, who have an excellent band and uniforms like toy soldiers of a hundred years ago; the Swiss Guard, dressed in magnificent red-yellow costumes of the sixteenth century; and the gendarmes of the police, in grand Napoleonic uniforms. A French gentleman who condescends to speak Italian believes that he is giving a logical and exhaustive explanation of what's going on by saying that the Pope is *"un idola."* Not an idol, Sir—I answer—but a man like everyone else who has reached the holiness of his status and the greatest burden by an inspired process of selection. An old Frenchman with great whiskers and a goatee as in the times of Maupassant winks his eyes hearing my polite riposte: *"sont pas des catholiques, sont des curieux."*

Curiosity, naiveté, and impatience notwithstanding, and in spite of the small drawbacks that a crowd entails, the function of the new Dogma, for those people who did understand its significance, was the greatest and most trenchant event of the Holy Year.

The papal parade has continued for an hour when six hundred bishops appear, marching two abreast. Their white miters trailing across the square gradually design a milky way on the ocean of heads. Silver trumpets announce the arrival of the Pontiff. At that point the arguments, explanations, informations end abruptly. No one has anything to say: the questions and answers that filled three hours of waiting disappear, the presence of the Pope has the strength to absorb them all: *"Evviva il Papa! Evviva il Papa!"* There is only one person, only one voice in Saint Peter's Square.

And much more time elapses between the Pope's exit through the Bronze Door among the acclaiming crowd, and his arrival at the steps of the Church, where the throne has been set up. There, standing under the sky in the pulsing sunlight, he will proclaim:

Immaculatam Deiparam semper Virginem Mariam, expleto terrestris vitae cursu, fuisse corpore et anima ad caelestem gloriam assumptam.

Catholics in our age when confronted with dogma do not react or yield; they stay neutral, and receive it as one news item among others, as if it were a simple formality. It is as if they lacked the background needed in order to understand. It was the highest point of the Holy Year, the summit to be attained on that morning of All Saints. The prize, the great reward of those who had followed it in faith and fervor. The Pontiff's words flew over the square with a swish of wings, as if a multitude of doves had been released. One had only to close his eyes and let himself be carried away in an ecstasy of light. Instead, it became a perfect example of the contradiction inherent in our age, when man has learned to fly with his body only to forget the great flights of the soul. The people in Saint Peter's square looked like birds with severed wings.

Science in its amazing conquests, the mind in its almost infinite ways, have only limited, barred, and obstructed their search for a reality which doesn't exist, since everything is real and everything is unreal. What do I care if I fly like a sparrow or a finch if my mind remains that of the sparrow and the finch. Everything has been working against the imagination. Therefore the Ascension of the Virgin was acknowledged as run-of-the-mill news, rather than as an elating, almost consuming flame sparked of the soul. Yet our artists had never questioned this fact which uplifted, exalted them: no doubt crossed their mind as they saw Mary rise to Heaven all dressed— just go to the Church of the Friars and Titian will show you. How could he have painted her unless all his consciousness was living the purity, the reality of that image? And hundreds and thousands besides him; their work bears witness in hundreds, thousands of museums and churches. They really saw her rise, for them the supernatural event was a reality, otherwise today we wouldn't see it on those tablets and canvasses. The Dogma already existed for those men of grand imagination. If they had been on Saint Peter's Square the morning of All Saints, 1950, the proclamation of the Dogma would have been indeed a simple formality. Your three-engine, four-engine planes and Flying Fortresses have only tamed your flight, you are lost in clouds over the lands of mediocrity. Nor will machines allow you to find again those heights, your herculean effort can only push you lower and lower again. God has given man imagination, a machine that has no maximum altitudes, no limits, no boundaries; a machine whose engines cannot stall, nor do its propellers have ever to be repaired— imagination to reach any place, to reach Him without having to resort to factories.

"ALL
THIS
LIGHT!"

DON FILIPPO di Santo Ste-
fano, who had been standing on Saint Peter's steps with the
retinue of dignitaries surrounding the papal throne, closed his
eyes at the proclamation of the Dogma, dazzled by the light;
when he opened them again he felt as if his feet had lost contact with the ground. The great square and its cheering crowd,
the presence and passage of the Pontiff looked to him like a
dark tide whose shape and motions he could not follow. In his
ears he heard a vague and sweet humming, to which it was
so pleasant to yield.

Returning home in Via Monserrato, Checco noticed that the
Prince's face was unusually flushed and smiling, with a smile

never known before. Behind it his ever-present and ready thought seemed absent.

Checco helped him out of the costume, a task which took a disturbingly long time and was accomplished in a silence deeper than usual. He helped the master into his everyday black suit, or, rather, he dressed him.

As soon as he was dressed he began to wobble; his weakness and instability increased swiftly.

Checco made him lie down on the cot in his suit, and he stayed there staring above him, with a face over which color and smile expanded together. Fatigue, Checco thought, made itself felt at the end of that joyful year in which he had attended so many ceremonies.

Checco brought something to eat, but the Prince refused even a glass of milk. He answered the many concerned questions with monosyllables and hazy, sometimes incomprehensible words. They were always in the affirmative, as if to conceal the fact that he wasn't paying attention, or that he didn't understand the questions, and that it was difficult for him to move his mouth.

These signs suggested that he wasn't suffering but was only tired, so Checco thought that a good night's rest would be the surest remedy. He decided to put him into bed. The operation turned out to be very complicated and lengthy, each movement presenting a new problem. Small as he was, Checco found it difficult to handle a body so large, and more and more inert; the face which nature seemed to have made colorless became ever more flushed, and the flame-like smile gradually burned higher.

Checco never left the Prince's bedside that day, and stood by all night trusting that rest would be enough to restore his strength and health.

The Prince spent a quiet night, seeming to repose in absolute serenity, but never fell asleep.

At the coming of day, realizing that the lassitude grew deeper instead of diminishing, Checco went downstairs and asked Bice to go to the nearest phone to notify the children.

The first to arrive was the Mother Abbess, who had been already awake. A little later came Norina, whose eyes filled with tears at the sight of her father so different from always.

The two beautiful women, standing a little stiffly, one crying, the other praying, watched their father. One tear would have been enough to spoil the bearing of the Abbess, while Norina had only tears. The color of health was changing the Prince's features astonishingly, and the lethargy into which he had fallen seemed the sweetest condition.

Pulling herself together, Norina ran out to return within an hour with the Sequis' family doctor.

The physician patiently, carefully touched and listened to every part of the Prince's body, with the attitude of someone fulfilling a duty to the letter. On taking his leave, he called the women to one side to tell them that unfortunately there was nothing that could be done. The Prince might fall into a state of progressive coma and live some days, or perhaps only a few hours longer. He prescribed those balms and liniments that science offers to make man's end less painful. But anything could be read in the Prince's vacant face except pain.

Norina left for a second time, and returned in great haste with a nurse, who put on her white uniform and took charge of the patient.

Billy-Bet arrived toward noon. They seemed more resentful than sorry; they were surprised and uncomfortable. They were furthest from the idea of death, and its presence upset them physically.

The Prince watched everyone, smiling, his face still getting more red against the white of the pillow. He stared at each

186

person in turn, on the verge of saying something, then his eyes moved on to another, as if looking for someone who could make him speak. Then he turned to the ceiling and his eyes lingered there; at that point he seemed not to desire anything, he appeared to be satisfied as he was.

At vespers the priest of Santa Lucia brought the Eucharist and next morning, right after having said early Mass, the Extreme Unction.

At noon Don Filippo di Santo Stefano was visited by Cardinal A. R. M., a close friend and former schoolmate at the college of Mondragone. The Most Eminent Prelate carried a message with him: the special blessing of the Holy Father. The Prince looked at him for a long time without tiring. His eyes shone, they expressed what the tongue couldn't tell.

When everyone was gathered in the room, including the young priest who had had him for an acolyte so many mornings, His Eminence leaned over the kneeling-stool by the bed, under the great silver cross returned from a Crusade centuries ago, and began the prayers for the dying.

At one point the Prince, who seemed to be listening in a slumber, moved his eyes, tightened his mouth, and turning his head appeared to have resumed contact with the environment and consciousness of the people. He looked over every part of his room as if he had just seen it again after a long absence. They all crowded near the bed, surrounding the Cardinal: Checco and the Abbess, Norina, the priest of Santa Lucia. Billy-Bet stayed at a distance, close to the window, where once in a while they exchanged a few unrecognizable words. Or they walked up and down the entrance room in front of the papal throne, like sentries on duty. Death was for them an accident; and above all an unsettling and bothersome spectacle, basically rather unclean. They felt that it wasn't right to devote so much attention to it; the less said about it, the better. Bice

187

and Orazio, kneeling at the sides of the door, were two torch-bearing angels as they answered the prayers:

Proficiscere, anima christiana, de hoc mundo, in nomine Dei Patris omnipotentis, qui te creavit: in nomine Jesu Christi filii Dei vivi, qui pro te passus est: in nomine Spiritus Sancti, qui in te effusus est: in nomine gloriosae et Sanctae Dei Genetricis Virginis Mariae: in nomine beati Joseph, incliti ejusdem Virginis Sponsi. . . .

Two, three times did the Prince open his lips as if against strong resistance, and stared at the illustrious prelate in an effort to speak. He turned to each of them, and to each he addressed a fully conscious gesture of greeting. He made new and harder efforts to talk, and mumbled a few meaningless words to respond to the tension that the others centered on him. Then a violent, almost desperate attempt to join with his voice the prayer:

Deus misericors, Deus clemens, Deus, qui Secundum multitudinem miserationum tuarum peccata poenitentium deles, et praeteritorum criminum culpas venia remissionis evacuas: respice propitius super hunc famulum tuum, et remissionem omnium peccatorum suorum, tota cordis confessione poscentem, deprecatus exaudi.

For a short period he answered almost clearly:

Commendo te omnipotenti Deo, carissime frater et ei, cujus es creatura, committo: ut cum humanitatis debitum morte interveniente persolveris, ad auctorem tuum, qui te de limo terrae formaverat, revertaris. Egredienti itaque animae tuae de corpore splendidus Angelorum coetus occurrat. . . .

Until he was overwhelmed by a new exhaustion and the words garbled and disappeared from his lips. He turned from side to side impatiently looking for something to hold onto, his eyes glared violently when they recognized what he wanted. His arms shot out and grasped Checco's arm at the wrist, so hard that Checco felt as if it were breaking, and as he held it tightly while his body strove to arise, he said distinctly: "All this light!" His head fell on the pillow.

The red slowly left his cheeks, as the sun sets in the evening; the smile on his lips extinguished: the face returned to its natural pallor.

NOT
ONE
FLOWER

WE HAVE SPENT so much time in order to know, to learn, and to understand, yet we still do not know what death is. We do not know its true essence, its real meaning, its natural color, its value. Perhaps in far away times they did know such things, but they have escaped us and we don't remember them. The only thing we can do is to take it as it comes.

In the life of man there are only two absolutes: love, from which life originates; and death, in which life ends. Death is a conclusion, a crowning point: it belongs to life and is its last and greatest act. At whatever age it comes, death is not an accident; the broken column is a bad allegory for it. As heroes and martyrs show, life without death would be like a body without a head. It is therefore strange that while love gives joy to everyone, death should bring only sadness and pain. Is it because we love life so much, because we are so attached to it, that death appears sad to us? Yet life is beautiful because it ends, as all things that last a short time are beautiful. Life without end would be like a life sentence—a horrible punishment. It is death we have to thank for the highest joys; things that we now like would become odious: if death did not exist we would discover it sooner or later as the greatest boon to mankind. But just try to seem happy in the presence of a corpse, and see what will happen.

Although he had nothing to leave behind, Don Filippo di Santo Stefano still had his palace. His last property was in a desperate state of chronic disrepair; its lodgers were people living on the borderlines of destitution. The rent they had paid had been just enough to cover taxes and the expenses of the Prince's daily meals and those of his servants, who had many years ago forgotten the existence of an ancient custom called salary. And we know that such meals did not add to the volume of Checco's satchel. The only thing left at the family fief of Rovi—a magnificent castle surrounded by an endless expanse of fields—were the few square feet on which the chapel was built. This had been saved by law, and the family still held the privilege of being buried in it. Therefore the Prince's will was very short, consisting of a page and a half of writing; like the letters of people who can write only a few lines, each word of which drips sweat. So it will be easy for us to reproduce its main headings, and offer it as a document of morality.

The corpse had to be placed at the foot of the papal throne: "This being not an act of pride on my part, but one of devoted servitude."

He could have been dressed in the costume of Secret Chamberlain under that throne, the one he had worn in the suite of four Popes during almost half a century. Pius XII among them, his favorite: both had been Romans, born three years and only a few steps apart; he had followed his life in all its stages, up to the light of holiness.

He could have worn the scarlet uniform and the white cloak of the Knights of Malta. In his sleep under the papal throne the Prince could have worn many other splendid and distinctive costumes; in the papers, his obituary ran half the length of a page. Or he could have been dressed in the clothes that he had always worn, the ones he went to serve Mass in every morning at his parish—thin black tie and high stiff collar—the one he wore two or three times a year when, overcoming an inner resistance, he went out in high society to fulfill a fatherly duty. The old worn-out suit that, like a varnish, was one with his body, that the people of the neighborhood had long ago been accustomed to seeing without noticing, like the threads of rain or the rays of sunlight.

"I shall be clothed in the cassock of Saint Francis." It was so dressed that he had attended the functions in the church of Ara Coeli on the Capitol Hill, and had carried the cross on the Sundays of Lent. St. Peter's and Ara Coeli had been the two poles of his life: the first he approached as a Roman noble, the second as a beggar. Santa Lucia, his parish, was in the center. He had lived in those three stations, and for them.

"Around my body, I want no music, and not one flower."

This paragraph was so strong and harsh that it seemed to condemn two things that everyone likes and that are so beautiful.

"I have nothing to leave, my safe is empty. I want the cheapest funeral, the same as anyone who has nothing left. And I shall be transported on the least expensive vehicle available . . . ."

192

As for a moral lesson, the Prince of Santo Stefano limited himself to a few words at the end of his testament:

"With death the earthly accounts are closed, any word beyond it is superfluous. Acts only matter; man counts inasmuch and according to how he acts."

After having read the document three, four times with eyes full of tears, Norina went home to bring the news to her mother-in-law, who was waiting impatiently.

Mrs. Sequi was at her desk, typing some letters. When Norina entered she took off her glasses and moved the armchair in a position from which she could listen better.

"No music and no flowers."

Mrs. Sequi seemed to be talking to herself:

"A little bit of music does a lot of good in certain cases: it helps to keep your spirits up, it muddles your thoughts a little. It's good for the dead, too, they seem to come alive. . . . But if he doesn't want it, he won't have it. No flowers. Imagine if such a thing is possible, I leave it up to you. Our business associates, friends, acquaintances will all send wreaths; you know it very well. It would be very hard on the florists, especially since they get rid of their worst stuff for the dead. Can you imagine the curses they will send the extravagant old man. Saints scare me more than the devil. What has he achieved with all his poverty? Just a lot of trouble, and some of it will be hard to straighten out. You can't fight poverty with hand-outs . . . of course if I get someone who is hungry I'll run to the kitchen and bring him some food. But this only makes poverty grow, it encourages the lazy and the inept; what we need is work, new activities, industries and traffics. We need to find work for everybody, jobs to give everyone a respectable life. It's amazing that some people should like such a thing as poverty."

Her eyes red from crying, Norina looked outside the window

distraughtly. She was incapable of taking a stand between her father's will and the comments of her mother-in-law. She had loved her father with childish sweetness. Despite his character and his way of life he had been the only person with whom she felt completely at ease, without needing to pretend or to lie. She did not love her mother-in-law, for whom she entertained an insuperable, inborn dislike; yet she agreed with her opinions.

"Can you remember exactly what the will says?"

Norina looked like a little girl reciting her lesson to the teacher.

"Around my body . . . not one flower."

"Well, well."

Mrs. Sequi furrowed her brows, which solved the most intricate problems with a stroke of genius.

"Around," she cried. "Are you sure? Did he really write 'around'?"

"Yes, around."

"So what will we do? We'll keep quiet. Let them send wreaths; the more, the better. As they arrive, we'll have them placed on the first floor and the courtyard, none will go upstairs—around the body there won't be any flowers. And we'll send them behind him at the funeral. He hasn't written that he doesn't want them behind. And the cheapest possible transport. I'm ready to send over a garbage-cart if it's needed." She stood up, refreshed by her good judgment. "Nothing around, everything behind, we took care of him, too."

Checco dressed the master in the Franciscan cassock; Orazio shaved him for the last time, and combed his hair, still thick and not quite white. The corpse was laid in state beneath the throne, surrounded by four burning candles. The doors were opened.

The people of the neighborhood thronged in to look for the last time at the man whom they had watched for years without seeing. The long and thin man, gathered within the brown cassock in the pallor of death, under the red canopy and next to the golden armchair with the coat of arms of the Popes, was a sight never to be forgotten. Death had rekindled curiosity about him. Hereafter they would look over Via Monserrato as if a doorjamb or a gate were missing. A scent of holiness wafted around the room furnished only with a throne, four lighted candles, and the corpse of a prince dressed as a beggar. Little old women, scurrying about like mice, came and went, saying their prayers as if they were in church.

Friends, acquaintances and no end of clergymen came to visit the deceased. With a sleight of hand death had revealed a wide world around the man who seemed to have lived in oblivion and loneliness.

Checco had placed himself at the side of the corpse right from the beginning and hadn't budged from there.

Around one o'clock in the morning he remained alone with two nuns and some lay Franciscan brothers, who took turns during the all-night wake. Someone appeared on the threshold, stopping like a statue in the frame of the door. It was Gherardo, Duke of Rovi and now Prince of Santo Stefano: he stood absolutely still for a long time, staring from a distance at his father's body. Then he vanished in the same way he had come.

The funeral began at eleven o'clock the next morning.

A tattered horse-cart wobbled up to the palace gates, its sides all blotched and creased by the weather. Behind it began to arrive luxurious cars from which ladies and gentlemen alighted. At the two ends of Via Monserrato and on Piazza Farnese the police were having a hard time organizing and untying a jam of two hundred and fifty cabs and carriages carrying wreaths of flowers.

The casket was sealed and transported to the little cart that had been waiting for two hours on the street. The procession unfolded and began to move.

In the center of the first row, right behind the cart, walked Gherardo di Santo Stefano. Mrs. Sequi and her husband were on his right; on his left the Abbess, Norina and her husband Alberto.

Pia Sequi was in a very bad mood, nervous and listless. Incapable of hiding her feelings, she showed in her unease the difference between her beliefs and those of the deceased. There was something jarring in that ceremony, each detail out of tune with the rest. A crowd of distinguished men and of women covered with long black veils, some touching the ground; high prelates and important officials—all walking behind a dirty, run-down cart drawn by a hag whose ribs could be counted one by one, driven by a red-nosed old man with a cap on his head, who seemed to be leading a mule on a country trail—the only thing he lacked was a pipe in his mouth. It was something Mrs. Sequi could not appreciate, and she kept shaking her head and mouthing an eloquent, if silent, "no." She clenched her fists at every few steps, like a general who sees the battle take an undesired turn; not being able to use them on anyone, she shook them at the stones of Via Monserrato. How many times must she have repeated "dammit" to herself.

Only Norina felt real grief. Covered by a black veil from head to ankles, glad of being thus protected, she showed in her heavy steps an overwhelming pain. It took her great effort to keep a bearing of assured nobility and even more assured beauty. It was obvious that she would have wanted to shorten the ceremony as much as possible.

The Mother Abbess shone in patrician elegance under her coif, but her face was completely impassive: it suggested the wooden statues of saints and noblewomen carved centuries ago by Tuscan craftsmen with such refined ingeniousness.

As usual, Checco didn't obey the requirements of convention and ceremony; he walked at the side of the cart that carried his master. Alone, he followed him with unchangeable flat-footed steps, in no way different from every morning when they went to Mass together. His face could not be altered, and he followed him in death with the serenity with which he had followed him in life.

Orazio and Bice had wedged themselves in between the first and second rows. They didn't feel up to walking in the first, but they considered themselves above walking with the ordinary people behind them. In her priestly hat and garments, hands clutched on her breast, Bice stared at the sky, wishing to join her master. Poor Orazio fluttered at her side as if dying of cold, unable to do anything with his hands that had now lost their illustrious occupation.

Leonia Macuto was elegant and above reproach in weeds. Her magnolia-like paleness stood out warmer against the background of a funeral.

The half-blind Duchess of Ascoli was very worried about losing her escort, and kept repeating:

"Don't stray far, Gelsomino, stay close or we will not find each other in this commotion." She breathed more easily when she saw him at her side.

"Funerals aren't what they used to be; people really cried then, now they only pretend to."

"It seems to me that they don't even try to pretend any more."

"Last spring I was watching a funeral at Monte Carlo. . . ."

"The one of the fair Otero?"

"Of course not, Otero is still alive."

"They said she was dead at least a dozen times."

"Everybody has become used to ugly women, these irresponsibles have no idea of what feminine beauty is. Otero is alive more than ever, but she isn't at Monte Carlo any more, she has a villa in Antibes. People who call on her claim she is as beautiful as she was seventy years ago."

The Marquess Terribili had buttonholed a young newsman: "All this fuss for an old fanatic. If a woman of genius had died they wouldn't make one-fourth of this noise. I can't understand why my friend Sequi, who is so intelligent, doesn't see it. This man was a nobody, a total loss. . . ."

The Duchess delle Fratte every now and then exclaimed to the painter Fiorelli, who escorted her: "My God, death is so horrible. How sad! How horrible! Why does one have to die? It's so nice to live. . . ." Shivers ran through her like waves through the sea. One could see that she needed a strong and warm support to cheer her up, but given the circumstances this was impossible. Fiorelli tried to do as much as he could, telling her that he couldn't stand death either, but that for some strange reason it had the same effect on him as making love did—it made him terribly hungry. As soon as he got home he would eat like a wolf. "Go away," answered the Duchess, "go away, leave me alone." "It's a vicious circle really, because after eating I have to make love right away." "I told you to go away, please, do go." "Yes? . . . Should I go?" asked Fiorelli, coming closer to give her courage and strength, "Must I really go?" "I will never again go with you to something serious." "Do these things seem serious to you?" "For God's sake, leave me alone."

Baroness Costanza had come with Ali. But as soon as they left the car to enter the palace Ali was overcome by terrible anxiety, he began to shake so that the Baroness had to take him away immediately: "Let's go, my joy, my only treasure, this stuff is not for you." She would apologize in person to Mrs. Sequi. She would without doubt answer: "I can't say you were wrong because I was more upset than you were. At least you could leave, while I couldn't."

Then came representatives of religious orders and charitable associations, the Knights of Malta in high uniforms, officers, priests, nuns, and some more distinguished ladies and gentlemen.

It had been impossible to hold the ceremony in the parish church of Santa Lucia. There were several hundreds of people, and there just wouldn't have been enough room for them. So the service took place in Sant' Andrea della Valle, the old church of the Farnese: no music, not even the sound of the organ; only Gregorian chant punctuated the chillingly simple ritual. Since the morning had been gray and cool, one of those mornings that in Rome hint at winter long before it comes, all the ladies had on fur coats. A merchant who saw them walk by his store on Corso Vittorio swore that if he had a billion lire and if the furs had been for sale, he would have bought them on the spot and made an excellent deal.

Billy-Bet were not in evidence. They kept away as if they had been unrelated to the deceased, merged in the back of the crowd. Close to each other, they looked mistrustful and displeased. This was not their kind of a show; they weren't made for it and it made them feel humiliated, diminished, reduced to nothing. They detested everything sad, even the pretense of sadness that many enjoy; they liked places where one could laugh openly and at all times. They knew how to laugh so well that it was a form of art: without it they couldn't be sure of their existence. It was a shame not to be able to laugh a little here too, after all it might have not been out of place— and it was such a waste, because they had a good laugh just ready between their teeth.

BROTHER
GIOCONDO

WHENEVER some weighty problem urgently needed to be solved, Mrs. Sequi was ready to display her constructive abilities. She walked up and down before the desk in her studio, with manly steps; arms behind the back and fingers nervously playing, or clenched across the breast.

This day was extremely important.

Things were in good shape and well directed, they only needed a last stroke of genius to settle them, crowning her intricate strategy. At stake was the rescue of the Santo Stefanos, whose ship had been leaking on every side.

With her son's marriage she had considered herself also

wedded to the cause of that original family. A cause she hadn't been able to help, frustrated year in and year out by the personality of the old Prince: retiring, obstinate, unbending—he had been adamant towards any compromise or arrangement. It had taken all her resolution and ability, but now things were in good shape and well directed.

After the Prince's death, Gherardo di Santo Stefano was received in a very private audience by the Holy Father. Falling on his knees he admitted and regretted his faults; the careless, messy life he had led for such a long time, and asked for forgiveness.

Everyone knows how happy the Holy Father is in a case of this kind; his fatherly heart is always deeply moved. The lost sheep returning to the fold is welcomed with open arms, as in the Scriptures the prodigal son was received with honor and feasting. Aware of what the life of Gherardo's father had been, the Pope showed complete understanding and mercy to the son.

His marriage to Magda, the Syrian dancer, was to be immediately annulled as an impossible aberration, so the young Prince would soon regain his freedom on that score. Luckily they didn't have children, which made the proceedings easy and fast. Since young Santo Stefano had spent his carefree life abroad, where it was difficult to evaluate the gravity of his actions, his misbehaviors remained enveloped by the fog that covers distances. The consensus was that they had been mistakes due to an exceedingly vigorous youth, and should be forgotten; traces of his action would not remain even in memory: his new exemplary life would sponge them out. Having made these points, the Holy Father opened his arms to the new Prince of Santo Stefano, his Secret Chamberlain.

After his visit to the Pope, Gherardo was supposed to call on the Sequis, where the lady of the house was anxiously awaiting him. She walked up and down her studio, stopping

201

at the window overlooking the garden; but she didn't notice the trees and flowers.

The clock on the fireplace sounded three o'clock. Turning towards it Mrs. Sequi unconsciously counted the strokes. Shortly afterwards a servant announced:

"His Excellency, the Prince of Santo Stefano."

"Let him in," she answered in a determined, masculine tone.

Gherardo was all dressed in black. His healthy and cheerful face looked aggressive in mourning. He kissed the woman's hand, and sat down next to her on the sofa whose expansive softness was more flattering than comfortable.

It was difficult for both of them to begin.

For the Prince because, willy-nilly, he was in a position of inferiority with respect to this woman whom he despised from the heights of his unalterable birth, and whose superiority he would not acknowledge. For her it was difficult because she knew that today she had to weigh and measure her words, so that one too many would not break all the eggs in the basket. An unusual caution she did not relish, but which she resorted to when necessary.

With inspired shrewdness, Mrs. Sequi started on a jokingly familiar tone, which would make it easier for him to express himself. She patted him chummily on the knee.

"Everything's for the best, I understand."

"The annulment will take a very short time. The other party being an alien, in three or four months it will be over. Perhaps even less."

"Of course, where His Holiness shows a personal interest in something . . ." she winked at him. "And what did she have to say about it?"

"She took it well. At first she had a fairly violent reaction, which is only natural, but when she understood that there was nothing for her to do, she claimed to be happy about it. To tell the truth, after having lived together in perfect harmony for three years, from the day we were married on our relations changed from this to that." The Prince turned the palm of his hand upside down.

"It happens all the time."

"She found Rome terribly heavy and stuffy, a boorishly provincial town where it was impossible for her to live."

"I wouldn't argue that it's very amusing here, on the other hand one doesn't live only for amusement. It depends what kind of a life you can organize for yourself, in this sense it's like any other place. Being a Roman, you are unaware of the acclimatization that we outsiders have to suffer through."

For a brief period of silence Mrs. Sequi seemed to be thinking.

"So in a few days you'll be a young bachelor again."

Gherardo laughed, and so did the woman, even louder.

"A seasoned bachelor."

"Not at all! You don't look older than twenty-seven or twenty-eight. You Romans don't spoil your foreheads with thinking, you stay as young as you want to be. Perhaps you are right. Everyone is right, it depends on the point of view and what we were born with." She went on cautiously; they were reaching a crucial point and she had to cross a bridge without knowing the strength of its supports. But being a brave woman, she went on:

"Yes, you are still young. But as the head of the family you have to decide yourself."

Gherardo looked at her with a widening smile, the woman's frankness put him in good humor. Only his father had ever been able to make him lose his temper and the inborn optimism of his character; Mrs. Sequi on the other hand had the ability of overcoming his resistances, of blunting his edges, of making him laugh.

"It's time for a wife," she threw down her card with a giggle, to keep the game on the right track. "A real wife, with the prerequisites that you need."

"Well, it's not easy."

"Who says so?"

"I do."

"I promise you it's very easy. Do you want to see?"

Gherardo watched her in silence while she quickly stood up and ran to open a drawer of her desk. She returned with one hand behind her back hiding something very important. With an adorable expression, between mystery and roguishness, she extended three snapshots:

"Give a look at these."

Gherardo took them, looked them over, and kept going from one to the other with obvious interest. But he wouldn't say a word.

"Well? What do you think?"

He lifted his head, and finally answered:

"But she's a child."

"Fresh stuff, don't you think?"

"How old is she?"

"Twenty."

"I will be forty in a short while."

"So what?"

"So it means that now it may be all right, but in ten years she'll be only thirty, and I fifty."

"It's not the critical age, that comes later. However, you will be smart enough to allow your wife's beauty a dignified sundown."

After having watched her thoughtfully, Gherardo went back to looking at the pictures, one by one.

"She's really pretty."

"What did I tell you? She isn't even a flower yet, she's

204

just a bud. Look at the mouth. Could you imagine a thinner one? It's less than half an inch. I would like to be in your shoes for one night. Why not? I wouldn't mind being that little girl for one night, or maybe two."

Gherardo laughed wholeheartedly. Even when proud, a Roman is easy to get along with.

Mrs. Sequi lifted an arm and smacked him across the back.

"Enjoy each other, while you are young and able."

"What's her name?"

"Anna. But at home everyone calls her Nini. Imagine, there are four brothers, three of them married, and all they were able to produce was this little slip of a girl. They all married late, with older women. Her father is my age, we are childhood friends. Everything they own will go to Nini, by joint agreement of all four brothers."

"Where is she from?"

"Milan."

"What's her father doing?"

"He owns big business."

Gherardo could not hide a revealing movement, so he started to laugh, feeling actually more comfortable now that his hand was discovered. He said jokingly:

"Sausages, in all likelihood."

"Worse than that."

"Nails."

"Laxatives."

They laughed together in good friendship.

"They have a very lucrative chemical and pharmaceutical company. It's the line to be in now. They make millions by the bushel. They own textile factories and a host of minor firms. First-rate after the war. All this abundance is too heavy a burden for the shoulders of a little girl; only a prince could help her to bear it."

Gherardo didn't know what to do; kept looking again and again at the pictures he held with a lively pleasure.

"But what does she think?"

"When they told her she may become a princess she couldn't sleep for three nights."

"Poor thing."

"She will get over it, don't worry. Perhaps you can sing her a lullaby to make her sleep. She wanted to see her prince, and when she saw your pictures that Norina and I sent her, she broke out in tears."

"She thought I was too old."

"On the contrary, she was crying for joy, she wouldn't stop. Boys don't interest her, she likes mature, grown-up men; she can't stand boys. When I was fifteen I couldn't stand boys either, I thought they were worse than flies. I used to be fascinated by men in their fifties, so busy and responsible. We are so silly when we are young."

"Later you changed your mind."

"By God."

"But...."

At this point Gherardo seemed to have chosen a neutral stand.

"But what? You have doubts? If you see any problems, we'll try to solve them."

"Does she want to come to Rome?"

"She's happy to."

"And where would we live?"

"In your palace."

Gherardo's brow clouded:

"But it's so gloomy."

"I will take care of making it cheerful. When I take charge, sadness disappears: it's afraid of me. You won't recognize your palace. I'll go first thing tomorrow to see what can be done to that hovel."

"The second floor is dreary, only to think of it I feel chills run down my bones. Yet I was born and lived in there until I was twenty-three. If we are going to have children we can't keep them in the dark."

"On the other hand it's your palace, you can't change it for another, and a modern house like this wouldn't do for you. It has a different tone. You should live on the last floor; if the present one can be adapted we will use that, or else we'll build a new floor on top of it. The palace is run-down only on the surface, I'm sure the walls and foundations are sound, it's all stone. An attic with balconies and a roof-garden where children can play in the sunlight most of the day. You can use the second floor for entertaining, with a small elevator to run all the way up. And that too will be altered and rebuilt as it should be."

"I don't think the throne can be moved."

"And who would think of doing that?"

Alarmed, Mrs. Sequi raised her arms, fingers outstretched:

"It should be kept like a petal of rose. It's sacred, it belongs to history. It has to stay there, in its own frame. In between, there will be two apartments that after being remodeled you will be able to rent to whomever you like."

"Shrimps will whistle before all this happens."

"In spring, we'll go to Milan for the wedding."

"What about the lodgers who live in the palace now?"

"They'll leave."

"But they can't be evicted. It's the law."

"My husband has just finished building some housing developments at Porta Latina, Monte Mario, and the Nomentano districts. They only have to choose, you'll see how fast they'll be going as soon as we show them those nice new homes. We haul them there lock, stock and barrel, all expenses paid. It's only a question of applying a little grease at the wheels, my

207

friend, you'll see how things will run along. In the next few days several of our building teams would be unemployed, it's a great opportunity to keep them busy. We'll send over as many as you wish. And if they don't finish in time you can stay a few more days on your wedding trip. After all, it's best to stretch the honeymoon as long as possible; it comes only once. I will send over so many workers that you'll see the palace change day by day. And the wedding by spring."

Gherardo sighed:

"Of course, at forty one can't waste time."

"And as far as politics go, it couldn't be better. Her family runs like clockwork. The girl's father, oldest of the four brothers, is a Christian Democrat; the second is a liberal, but goes to church; the third was a rabid Fascist, I think he still has some vivid memories—where there has been so much fire, the ashes stay warm. He's very patriotic, very nationalistic. The fourth one is funny, a non-conformist who lives alone in furnished rooms. He's a Communist and doesn't work, he is not concerned with the family business and just takes his share of the profits. He is involved in labor disputes and reads Marx. The family considers him the poor relation, the country cousin."

"He won't approve of such a wedding."

Mrs. Sequi looked at him with a smile that by now he was getting accustomed to:

"I'm sorry, but you haven't guessed right. When he heard that his niece would become a princess he began to dance for happiness. They couldn't make him stop. He has always adored that girl. Every time her parents invited him to dinner when she was small, he would bring her the biggest and most beautiful doll, the most beautiful ones she has were given by the Communist uncle. He must have given her more than a hundred dolls. He's an inveterate bachelor, and has agreed that his share would go to Nini, Princess Nini. But even if, God forbid, he were to get married, the others' would be plenty. Excellency, you have nothing to worry about."

She walked Gherardo to the stairs and they parted pleasantly, more like friends than relatives.

Re-entering her studio, Mrs. Sequi walked to the window before sitting back at her desk. She took in a healthy breath of air that filled her lungs: her plan was on the move. It made her feel satisfied down to her guts. She and her old friends would now be linked by family ties. They were clever people, the kind she liked, with whom they could understand each other just by moving a finger. They had absorbed business with their mother's milk, it was their only occupation from morning to night, even at night they made deals because they could only dream of business. Without having anything specific in mind yet, she envisioned new well-paying combinations, fat deals rising over the horizon. Business was like cherries, one brought up the next one; unforeseen developments popped up on every side. Business could multiply like the sands of a beach: manufacturing, building, contracts, financing, real estate, merchandising, politics, high-level marriages—the world she liked, the waters she liked to sail. She breathed deeply, satisfied: "The Holy Father is a saint and he can do whatever he wants; I am not a saint so I can't work miracles, but I can still do something, and when money is involved, I don't do badly at all." She sat at her desk, put on the glasses and went back to work.

Next morning Gherardo forced himself to climb up the stairs of his father's house.

Walking through the gate he felt a cape of lead fall over his shoulders, the walls seemed to push him back. At one side of the lodge Bice sat knitting, from the movement of her lips one could see that she was praying at the same time. She stood up with an empty expression of formal respect. Like a porcupine, she rolled herself up into a ball that the new master could not touch. After such a long absence she couldn't figure out what kind of a bird he was, and from things she had heard, there were reasons to keep one's distance. Her master was up there, if she lifted her eyes to Heaven she could see him dressed in gold and silk, the white feather on his hat and the sword at his side. She could see him in the midst of a host of other gentlemen dressed like him, in regal costumes strewn with precious stones; around them fluttered golden-haired angels and seraphim in pink and blue robes. Even from such a distance she was able to tell him apart from everyone else, and as soon as they would meet again she would greet him with the usual reserve, a restraint that, instead of chilling her, made her feel the strength of their relationship, their unconditional solidarity. Outwardly so cold, their greeting revealed the perfection of feeling that united them, more closely and firmly than any outburst of emotion could do.

Climbing the stairs, Gherardo was thinking: How can Mrs. Sequi make this place livable? Extensive, careful restoration may return to it the nobility of past centuries, but in those times the architects did not think about light, while today men want the sun inside their homes. How could his be filled with light, so that the musty smell and the prison-like gloominess would disappear? The only way out was to build on the roof; the roof was it.

He waited before ringing, as if he were not the owner of the house returning home. It seemed to him that he was waiting at the door to ask for something, and wondered anxiously whether his requests would be granted.

Checco came to let him in. He had a broom in hand; he had been sweeping the throne room.

"Come in, young master, you did well to come," he said very simply, but without any warmth.

Gherardo looked around the titanic hall in whose icy emptiness the great canopy stood out, the one under which he had seen his father in the sleep of death between four burning candles. He felt shivers running through him, as if the blood in his veins had turned to water. After having crossed the great hall, he hesitated before entering the room; he had to clench his fists and bite his lips in order to gain strength. Everything was in order. The small iron bed with a white blanket covering a mattress and a pillow. Next to it the kneeling-stool with the great silver cross brought back by a Santo Stefano from the crusades, the only object of value the Prince had kept. The desk, the ivory crucifix, nothing else. The sofa of peeling leather, broken and bumpy, seemed to be standing there in order to intimidate haunches. Two stools and the unfriendly arm-chairs looked at him with evil stares. Gherardo stood still and rigid, searching for his father's shape sitting in front of him during their last conversation. The chest of drawers was bare; on the center of the round table there was a bottle of blue glass with a little water inside, and a small dish with salt. He looked around still and stiff while Checco stood at the door with the broom in his hand, like a sentry.

After having thus brooded, he collected some courage, but the need to warm up the environment made him raise his voice a bit too much:

"How are you, Checco?"

"I'm fine."

Gherardo looked closely at him, as if he had never seen him before.

"I've cleaned here already, by tonight I'll have finished the big room too."

When it's difficult to say something, one always comes up with the most pointless and disconnected things, told in forced tones.

"Daddy's dead."

"Daddy's dead," answered Checco, then added: "He's dead and I'm still alive."

"You aren't sorry, are you?"

"One by one we all have to die."

Checco's serenity succeeded in quieting down his own excitement, and his tone became caressing:

"Was he angry at me?"

"Nope, he wasn't angry at nobody."

"After what we told each other last time I thought he might be."

"He knew all the time how it would end."

"Yes? Are you sure?" There was a new liveliness in Gherardo's voice.

"Didn't you know? He was sure that it would be this way."

"You'll stay with us, of course."

"No, Sir."

"Where will you go?"

"To the monastery, to be a friar."

"To the monastery? Which one?"

"To the one at Ara Coeli. His Excellency has left a fund for me there."

"Are you happy? Will you like it there?"

"Yessir. If it wasn't for your daddy, I would have gone there when I was a boy."

"You used to like me."

"I still do, very much."

"Then why are you going away, why do you leave me?"

"Because we agreed with the master. He knows it and sees what I'm doing."

"You said that Daddy wasn't angry at me. So he would be pleased too, if we stayed together."

"Nossir; because Daddy and I decided so."

"We won't make you do anything. You'll do whatever you

like. When our first child starts walking you'll take him out."

"But I want to do what I can, at the monastery I'll have to work, just as I did here."

"Think it over, Checco, before you decide."

"It's been decided a long time ago, between me and the master. Now I finish sweeping and tomorrow I'll go to the monastery. I'll leave the keys with Missbice, they'll be there whenever you want them."

"Aren't you sorry to be leaving this house where you have always lived?"

"No, because now I have to go. When I'm up there, I'll be closer to your daddy."

From the very dawn the morning was revealed as a day radiant with sunlight. One of those November days in which one can breathe in Rome the nostalgic beauty of summer.

As soon as he awoke, Checco settled the covers of his cot, and put everything in order in the little room. He made a parcel of his few belongings and bound them in a black scarf. He closed the windows, and with the package under his arm descended the stairs. At the entrance—the gates were still locked—he called Miss Bice to give her the keys. Running out to meet him, Bice bowed deeply, instead of greeting him as she used to: he wasn't any more her master's servant whom one could treat with familiarity. A few hours hence he would dress in the monastic cloth and become Brother Giocondo of Saint Francis' lay order; she was so overcome with emotion that she wasn't able to say a word. When Checco reached the door, ready to leave, she followed him with a shout:

"I'll come for Christmas Mass."

"Good-bye, Missbice."

He left as he always did, towards the Campo dei Fiori where he used to buy the bread. Instead of the satchel under his arm, he carried all he owned in a black scarf. He walked with his flat step, close to the walls. The street was empty. Here and there the sound of a window opening with forced eagerness. In front of Santa Maria di Monserrato, the church of the Spaniards, he tipped his hat. A young man whistling on a bicycle cut across the street like an arrow. In Piazza Farnese Checco didn't turn a glance at the regal splendor of the palace he left behind, yet he heard the waters in the great lilied fountains lull with their vibration the metaphysical void. He turned at Via dei Baullari and, reaching Campo dei Fiori, he heard here and there across the square the sound of lumber being tossed about: the more ambitious produce-sellers were assembling their stalls. Without glancing at them either, he went on through Via dei Giubbonari. Passing by San Carlo ai Catinari he again tipped his hat. He met a car on Largo Arenula, and in Piazza Mattei he responded to the gently dribbling water of the Turtle's fountain. By Via dei Funari he reached Santa Maria in Campitelli, and here for the last time Checco uncovered his head, before turning around Teatro Marcello into the Via del Mare. He was now at the foot of the Capitol Hill, at the bottom of the Ara Coeli staircase: alone. Just before beginning the climb he stopped and turned around:

I believe in God, the Father Almighty, creator of Heaven and earth ...

The sun was already shining in the sky, touching the earth with light: the top of monuments, of palaces, of houses. Marble and stone was changed into crystal.

And in Jesus Christ His only Son, our Lord,

According to his law he had lived, in it he wanted to die. He began to climb.

Who was conceived by the Holy Ghost ...

In that impressive loneliness, a burst of bells descended down to him from the church on the hilltop.

... born of the Virgin Mary, suffered under Pontius Pilate;

was crucified, died, and was buried.

The pains of man, his mistakes, his faults had to be ransomed with the blood of an innocent, because only an innocent has the power of redeeming them.

He descended into Hell; The third day He arose again from the dead; He ascended into Heaven,

Very slowly he climbed the endless staircase, and each step felt lighter under his tread.

sitteth at the right hand of God the Father Almighty;

At the top of that hill he would be reunited with the man who in life had been his spiritual father.

from thence He shall come to judge the living and the dead . . .

Peace to the living, to all those who fight, suffer and love on the earth, and for the dead everlasting happiness in Heaven.

I believe in the Holy Ghost . . .

In that spirit which prevented him from feeling tired at the ascent. That staircase had never seemed so easy to climb, not even when he had been a young man.

the holy, catholic Church . . .

The church was up there, its doors open, calling him with the sound of its bells that brushed against his forehead.

the communion of Saints . . .

The heavenly host whose acts and deeds live on, to help us reach them.

the forgiveness of sins . . .

Lord, before entering Your house I ask again Your mercy for the evil I might have done in thoughts or deeds.

The resurrection of the body . . .

So that even this poor body of mine might be changed into heavenly matter.

and life everlasting.

To which he would fly from the summit of that hill.

He had walked up the 124 steps without a pause, without

turning around. But when he reached the church, before entering its doors, he did turn around. The sun radiated over sky and earth, sparking diamond shivers among the green of the trees. The city throbbed in the sparkling light: its thousand-year-old ruins pulsated. Like chasms they gave a feeling of vertigo to the senses. He turned his gaze around to give a last look at the world; one step beyond the door and Checco would not be any more. Awash with sunlight, the domes of Rome seemed to be made of gold. From the dome of Saint Peter's, the farthest, to that of Gesù, which rose directly beneath, and all the others that he felt around him: Sant' Andrea della Valle, Sant' Agnese, San Carlo ai Catinari and San Carlo al Corso, Santa Maria in Vallicella, Santa Maria della Pace, Santa Maria del Popolo, I Fiorentini. . . . From each one the bells raised a shout of hope. He waited some more before taking that step, seeing as much as he could of the city which he had under his eyes and inside his heart. The city that taught him how to live, where he had found joy and pain; he looked all over it to include everything in an embrace. Roma, Roma, Roma, Roma: young and decaying, poor and billionaire, intimate and lewd, narrow and boundless.